I0603175

KENT'S HONOR

THE AEGIS NETWORK: JACKSONVILLE DIVISION

JEN TALTY

JUPITER PRESS

This book is a work of fiction. Names, characters, places, and incidents are products of the author's imagination or used fictitiously. Any resemblance to actual events or locales or persons living or dead is entirely coincidental.

Publishing History:

This book was initially published in Kindle Worlds and then with Aces Press as part of the, Special Forces: Operation Alpha World.
It was originally titled *BURNING SKIES*.

Copyright © 2018 by Jen Talty All rights reserved.
Updated Copyright © 2024 by Jen Talty All rights reserved.

No part of this work may be used, stored, reproduced or transmitted without written permission from the publisher except for brief quotations for review purposes as permitted by law. This book is licensed for your personal enjoyment only. This book may not be re-sold or given away to other people. If you would like to share this book with another person, please purchase an additional copy for each recipient. If you're reading this book and did not purchase it, or it was not purchased for your use only, please purchase your own copy.

PRAISE FOR JEN TALTY

"*Deadly Secrets* is the best of romance and suspense in one hot read!" *NYT Bestselling Author Jennifer Probst*

"A charming setting and a steamy couple heat up the pages in a suspenseful story I couldn't put down!" *NY Times and USA today Bestselling Author Donna Grant*

"Jen Talty's books will grab your attention and pull you into a world of relatable characters, strong personalities, humor, and believable storylines. You'll laugh, you'll cry, and you'll rush to get the next book she releases!" Natalie Ann USA Today Bestselling Author

"I positively loved *In Two Weeks*, and highly recommend it. The writing is wonderful, the story is fantastic, and the characters will keep you coming back for more. I can't wait to get my hands on future installments of the NYS Troopers series." *Long and Short Reviews*

"*In Two Weeks* hooks the reader from page one. This is a fast paced story where the development of the romance grabs you emotionally and the suspense keeps you sitting on the edge of your chair. Great characters, great writing, and a believable plot that can be a warning to all of us." *Desiree Holt, USA Today Bestseller*

"*Dark Water* delivers an engaging portrait of wounded hearts as the memorable characters take you on a healing journey of love. A mysterious death brings danger and intrigue into the drama, while sultry passions brew into a believable plot that melts the reader's heart. Jen Talty pens an entertaining romance that grips the heart as the colorful and dangerous story unfolds into a chilling ending." *Night Owl Reviews*

"This is not the typical love story, nor is it the typical mystery. The characters are well rounded and interesting." *You Gotta Read Reviews*

"Murder in Paradise Bay is a fast-paced romantic thriller with plenty of twists and turns to keep you guessing until the end. You won't want to miss this one..." *USA Today bestselling author Janice Maynard*

BOOK DESCRIPTION

Dixie sought refuge with her aunt in Jacksonville after her ex-boyfriend disappeared and stopped supporting their child. Her arrival coincided with her aunt's emergency departure to care for a friend, leaving Dixie to step into the role of nanny for Kent Carter, a single father struggling to manage his career and the care of his daughter. Kent, traditionally reserved and focused solely on his daughter, found himself unexpectedly drawn to Dixie.

However, as Kent delved into Dixie's background, hoping to understand the mysterious new nanny, his investigation inadvertently led her dangerous ex-boyfriend right to their doorstep. This reckless probe triggered a dire sequence of events, resulting in the kidnapping of both Dixie and Elle. Now, Kent must navigate a treacherous path, filled with peril and urgency, to rescue them both from an unforeseen threat that his own actions helped unleash.

NOTE FROM THE AUTHOR

Hello everyone!

It is important to note that this book was originally titled *Burning Kiss* and written as part of the Susan Stoker *Special Forces: Operation Alpha* world. Since the rights to the book have reverted back to me, I have stripped the story of all the elements from Susan's world (as it was legally required of me to do so) as well as changing the names of some of my characters so it would fit nicely into my Aegis Network series.

I have also expanded the story, adding scenes and updating a few things. I'm much happier with the storyline and characters now. I've always loved this series, but as with many things that I wrote years ago, I felt as though I could have done better.

Please enjoy!

Jen Talty

For the ones that came before.

WELCOME TO THE AEGIS NETWORK

The Aegis Network is the brainchild of former Marines, Bain Asher and Decker Griggs. While serving their country, Bain and Decker were injured in a raid in an undisclosed area during an unsanctioned mission. Instead of twiddling their thumbs while on medical leave, they focused their frustration at being sidelined toward their pet project: a sophisticated Quantum Communication Network Satellite. When the devastating news came that neither man would be placed on active duty ever again, they sold their technology to the United States government and landed on a heaping pot of gold and funded their passion.

Saving lives.

The Aegis Network is an elite group of men and women, mostly ex-military, descending from all branches. They may have left the armed forces, but the armed forces didn't leave them. There's no limit to the type of missions they'll take, from kidnapping, protection detail, infiltrating enemy lines, and everything in between; no job is too big or too small when lives are at stake.

As Marines, they vowed no man left behind.

As civilians, they will risk all to ensure the safety of their clients.

Kent Carter glanced at his watch. Going out with the guys often became a challenge of how often he'd check the time every thirty minutes. So, for the last half hour, it was six. Being a single father hadn't been easy. It was worse when he'd been in the military, leaving his precious little girl for weeks on end, worrying she'd forget who he was by the time he returned.

But now, the stress had become something entirely different.

"Hey." Rex nudged his arm. "Are you seriously worried about Elle while she's at my house with Tilly and Maren?"

"I'm not concerned about her well-being." Kent arched a brow. "I know she's having a ridiculous amount of fun playing mommy to Annabelle, Lucas, and Justice."

"Then what's the problem?" Rex arched a brow.

"My nanny has a family issue that came up last minute. She's sending her niece over tomorrow to fill in."

"Oh, I see." Rex nodded, tipping his beer. "How old is this girl?"

"An adult, but not the point. I don't know her or anything about her. I literally got the text an hour ago and we have training at the station and shit to do at the Aegis Network office all week."

"You have to relax, man." Rex slapped him on the shoulder. "Elle's what, ten now?"

"Don't remind me. She's growing up too fast and she wants to find me the perfect wife like yesterday."

Rex laughed. "She's been like that since she was two." He waggled his fingers. "Not to add any fuel to this fire, but she asked our next-door neighbor if she knew any young, nice-looking single women for her hot firefighter daddy."

"Sweet, Jesus. She didn't?" Kent shook his head.

Arthur leaned across the table. "Are we talking about cute, not so little anymore, Elle?"

"And how she wants to fix up her old man," Rex said.

"Hey, I know a dozen girls who wouldn't mind dating him," Buddy said, waving a chicken wing in the air. "But every time I ask him to go on a double date with me, he gives me some song and dance he doesn't have the sitter or doesn't want to leave Elle, which I totally respect. But, dude, you need to get out sometimes."

"What the hell do you think this is?" Kent glared.

"What I meant to say is you need to get laid." Buddy lowered his chin.

"You're an ass." Kent tossed a napkin in his direction.

"That might be the case, but everyone at this table doesn't disagree with him," Hawke said. "I mean, not to get too personal, but how long has it been?"

"None of your fucking business," Kent muttered. Hooking up with women had been a little easier when he'd been in the military. He could do it while deployed. It was meaningless sex and he'd never see them again.

Although, that did cause a bit of turmoil and guilt, for other reasons.

Now that he was a civilian, that part of his life was a little harder. He'd made a few friends that came with *benefits* over the years.

However, he'd also become bored with that kind of emotionless entanglement. None of them were the right person to introduce to his little girl. It wasn't that they weren't good enough. That wasn't even the point.

"You know, you've got a room full of guys absolutely willing to babysit so you can find yourself a woman." Garth raised his beer to his lips.

"I second that idea." Duncan nodded.

"Why don't you two idiots find your own ladies and let me worry about my love life, thank you very much." Kent lifted his wrist.

Rex pushed his arm down and glared. "Is something else besides the new nanny issue bothering you?"

"Honestly, it's just a combination of the new sitter situation and some things that Elle's going through that I'm not sure how to handle." Kent fiddled with the food on his plate. Becoming a father had been the best thing that had ever happened to him, even if it had also been the scariest. He loved Elle with every fiber of his being. She was the air that he breathed. Life didn't matter without her.

"I can't imagine my sweet little Annabelle becoming a young lady. I want to lock her up and throw away the key," Rex said.

"That's not going to solve any of that child's boy problems." Arthur smacked his head. "She's already informed me and Maren that she's going to be our daughter-we-wa, and then went into great detail in what that meant." He shook his head. "She told me someday she was going to make me a grandpa. I damn near died laughing."

"It's not funny." Rex lifted an onion ring and tossed it at Arthur's face. "My daughter is not marrying your son. I don't care what our wives say."

"I don't know," Garth said. "They are cute-ass kids. Imagine that gene pool mixed—"

"Shut your trap before I shut it for you." Rex glared.

Kent chuckled. While the exchange was insanely humorous, he understood without a doubt why it got under Rex's skin.

"Listen, man." Rex tapped the table. "I might not have any good advice to offer with whatever Elle is going through, but I'm a good listener."

"I appreciate that." Kent nodded. He might as well talk with someone. "She's always been a bit of a homebody. She worries about me and who's taking care of me. I keep trying to tell her that her old man can handle himself. But she sees the other kids at school and all the moms coming in to help. I do what I can, which is more than most dads, but lately, she's been withdrawn at school. She doesn't have a lot of friends, and even her teacher has noted that when they go out on the playground, she's either with the younger kids, by herself, or with the teacher aide. I'm worried about her."

"What does her teacher say?" Rex asked.

"That she'll keep an eye on her. That this is the time when girls start forming cliques and a clear popular group has been determined. Elle's not part of it, but when I ask Elle about those girls, she rolls her eyes and tells me they aren't the kind of kids she wants to hang out with."

"Smart girl," Rex said.

"This coming from the guy who was Mr. Popular wherever he went." Kent narrowed his stare.

"Yeah, but Tilly struggled with shit like that. She didn't always fit in with the kids at the country club or the rich girls at our school. They could be mean and often picked on Tilly," Rex said.

"I can't imagine anyone making fun of her. I wouldn't dare for fear of getting a high heel in my shin." The first time Kent had met Tilly, she'd marched onto Rex's boat, and a few weeks later, they were married.

Craziest thing, but looking at them now, it made perfect sense.

"Elle can talk with adults. Most kids her age don't know how to do that," Rex said. "It's a gift that will serve her well as she ages."

"I know." Kent didn't need anyone to tell him what a unique daughter he had. She was intelligent, resilient, and had a big heart. But that didn't stop him from losing sleep over how she preferred to spend time with him than making playdates, unless of course that friend's mom was single. "I want her childhood to be normal."

"It's as normal as it can be." Rex slapped him on the shoulder. "You're a great dad. You're always there when she needs you. And she has her crazy band of uncles." Rex squeezed. "I know you don't want to hear this, but having a lady in your life wouldn't be the worst thing in the world for Elle."

"I'm not going to bring women in and out of

her life. It will only confuse her and ultimately hurt her, especially if she gets attached, which she does so easily." Kent had been having this discussion a lot lately with what seemed like everyone. His nanny, Jackie, brought it up all the damn time, especially when he asked her to take Elle for the night, so he could meet up with one of his *friends with benefits*.

God, that sounded awful.

"Look, man, I understand your concern. I do. But she's the one leading the fight. Maybe you should listen," Rex said.

The waitress came by with the check. Finally, he could get the hell back to his daughter and stop with the chatter. He shouldn't have said anything to begin with.

"I'll call Maren and have her meet you at your place with Elle," Arthur said. "Should take her about the same amount of time to get there."

"Sounds like a plan." He tossed in a couple of twenties. "I'll see all you assholes tomorrow."

"Drive safe," Buddy said, waving his hand over his head.

Kent made his way to the parking lot and his prize possession.

His Harley.

Outside of his daughter, it was his favorite fucking thing in the world. Riding it was almost better than sex.

Although lately, he wasn't even sure he knew what sex was anymore.

He flung his leg over the seat, lifted the kickstand, and turned the key, revving the engine. Music to his ears.

Easing out onto the main road, he took the corners tight, but not too fast. While he loved his bike, and he didn't wear a helmet, at least in the state of Florida where it wasn't required, he wasn't reckless. He drove the speed limit. Followed all the rules of the road and didn't do anything stupid.

At least not in his book.

But, as his mother often reminded him, he did live his life on the edge. He had two risky jobs. One with the Aegis Network and the other as a firefighter.

Before that, he'd been in the Air Force. Although he'd had one foot out the door four years ago when Arthur approached the entire team about a unique opportunity.

It took all of ten minutes for him to arrive at his house. No one had the kind of funds that Rex and his wife had. But Kent's financial situation was always a struggle. He'd grown up dirt poor and his parents couldn't help him at all after high school. Whatever Kent wanted to do, it was on him and he completely understood. He didn't expect a handout and he certainly wasn't afraid of hard work.

Once in his driveway, he opened the garage and eased his toy—about the only thing he'd ever treated himself to—into the garage of his modest home. He lived about a half hour from everyone else, tucked away in a neighborhood that needed a lot of tender loving care. The homes were all in need of major repair. Some more than others. But it was a safe neighborhood. One that he didn't have to worry too much about his baby girl. And it was in an excellent school district because he couldn't afford a fancy private school.

Headlights flashed as Maren's SUV pulled into the driveway. She opened the driver's door. "Perfect timing."

"I'd say so," he said. "How was your night?"

"Wonderful. Tilly and I didn't have to lift a finger. Your daughter did everything except change diapers. I'm sure she could handle it, but Justice is at the age where he grabs his willy and runs away, thinking it's funny if something comes out of it."

He burst out laughing. "I'm sorry. I shouldn't find that funny, but I do."

"Yeah, well, Arthur thinks it's hysterical, and it doesn't help." Maren shook her head.

Elle stepped from the rear passenger side. "I tried not to crack up, Daddy. Really, I did. But when he peed all over the kitchen floor and slid across it like he was on ice skates, it was kind of hard not to."

Kent covered his mouth.

"It's okay. Go ahead. He's passed out cold and can't hear a thing." Maren wiggled her fingers. "Come give me a hug, Elle. Thanks so much for entertaining Justice and Annabelle so your aunt Tilly and I could have a grown-up evening."

"Anytime." Elle gave Maren a big hug. "I love playing with them."

"Thanks for driving her home." Kent waved before looping his arm around Elle. "Time for you to get washed up and ready for bed." He kissed her temple. She was getting so tall.

She glanced up with big doe eyes. "Did you have fun with the guys?"

"We had a blast."

"Did you meet any women?" She waggled her brows.

He ruffled her head. "It was boys' night. There was none of that. Now get ready for bed. When you're done, we can play a quick card game." He sighed, watching his daughter, who wasn't a baby anymore but wasn't a teenager yet, race up the porch steps.

She stopped and glanced over her shoulder. "I love you, Daddy."

"I love you too, Elle." He patted his chest. That right there was why he got out of bed every morning.

2

"**D**addy, why are you so worried about this stuff constantly?"

Out of the mouths of babes. Kent leaned against the railing of his porch, the weathered wood in desperate need of a paint job. He kept telling himself he'd do it next weekend, and then he'd find something more fun to do with Elle.

Maybe this could be a fun project to do together. As she kept reminding him, she wasn't his baby anymore.

"It's my job to worry, Buttercup."

Elle looked up at him from her perch on the steps and rolled her eyes. "Now that I'm ten, I'm too old to be called buttercup."

"Don't roll your eyes at me, young lady," he said with a smile as he sat down beside the little girl who had forever changed his life. "I hate it when you do that."

"I can't help it. It's what ten-year-olds do." She tilted her head and batted her thick eyelashes, her soft-blue eyes catching a ray of sunshine. Damn girl better never grow up, or he was going to be chasing off every young man with a shotgun.

He cringed at the thought.

He looped his arm around her shoulders. Her mother had only been five-five, but Elle was already five-two, so he suspected she would take after him. He hoped she stopped somewhere around five-ten, not six-three.

"I can see if someone can cover my shift today."

"Miss Jackie wouldn't send someone she wouldn't trust with her own children." Elle scrunched her nose and glared, as if mentally tossing daggers. "Besides, it's not like I'm two and need constant attention. You heard Aunt Maren. I was a big help last night and in a year, I can take the babysitting course and—"

"Stop trying to grow up on me," he said as he smoothed down her shoulder-length brown hair. "And you won't be babysitting until you're sixteen."

"I'll be too busy with my boyfriend by then, Dad."

He clutched his chest. "You're going to give your old man a heart attack."

She slapped her knee and burst out laughing.

"I don't see what's so funny."

He glanced at his watch, then down the street, lined with houses much like his—small, modest, affordable. There were big wheels, bicycles, and other toys in the front yards. He loved that about the area. Plenty of kids, when Elle decided she wanted to play with them, which lately wasn't often.

"You're like fifteen years younger than Heidi's dad. I think you're the youngest dad on the block."

"Actually, eighteen years younger, but who's counting…" His words trailed off as a young woman he'd never seen before turned the corner, pushing a little boy in a stroller. He swallowed. Hard. "Do you know that girl and her child?" he asked his daughter.

"No."

"Did you notice if anyone moved into Riley's place in the last couple of days?" The house had been empty for the past three months. Unfortunately, the neighborhood had a high turnover since these were considered starter homes. Someday,

Kent hoped to be able to afford a bigger home, but right now, he needed to save for Elle's college education.

"It looked empty when I walked by there the other day with Miss Jackie."

"Maybe she just moved in," he said, unable to tear his gaze from the beautiful creature strolling in his direction. His lungs burned for the oxygen he couldn't suck in.

The woman tucked a piece of blond hair that had fallen out of her long ponytail behind her ear in such a seductive manner that left him breathless. She held a piece of paper in her hand, and her gaze landed on the set of mailboxes as she padded by. The closer she got, the more his palms sweated and his pulse raced. He'd seen beautiful women before, but no one looked like the angel walking down the sidewalk, her long, bare legs striding behind the buggy. The way her muscles flexed every time her feet hit the pavement told him she had to be a runner.

He was a runner.

Maybe they could run together.

He should toss his libido out with the trash.

He'd date when Elle was in college. That would make him just shy of forty. Hell, lots of men started having kids at forty. Not that he wanted to, but his life would be far from being on the downhill side of things.

"Look, Mommy! A butterfly," the little boy in the stroller squealed as they passed his neighbor's driveway, getting closer to where he and his daughter sat.

"It's so pretty," the woman said with enthusiasm as she glanced at the paper.

"I want to get out." The boy twisted his body, looking over his shoulder. "Out, Mommy! Please!"

"When we find Mr. Carter's house, then you can get out. But you must be a good boy and stay next to Mommy, okay?"

Hearing his name snapped him back into reality. He blinked.

"I promise," the little boy yelled.

"She's pretty," Elle whispered.

His daughter certainly was perceptive.

"Stunning," he said softly. If he'd seen her in a bar, or anywhere, he'd want to ask her name. And it wasn't just about how incredibly sexy she was but also how she carried herself with a sense of confidence that Kent didn't see very often that made him contemplate tossing his rules out the window.

The woman's complexion bronzed under the

kiss of the sun. Her blue eyes twinkled, and she had the most adorable dimple on her right cheek when she smiled.

"I'm Mr. Carter." Kent stood, taking his daughter's hand. "But everyone calls me Kent."

"Hi. I'm Jackie's niece, Dixie. You must be Elle," Dixie said, reaching out her hand. Elle stood only a few inches shorter than Dixie. "My aunt talks nonstop about you."

"Is this her great nephew, Nicky?" Elle asked with the same excitement she had when he'd given her a cell phone for her birthday. "She has pictures of you on her fridge. You're even cuter in person." Elle leaned over and patted the boy's head.

"That's me!" The little boy danced in the stroller, tugging wildly at the strap over his middle. "Mommy! Out!"

"Say please." Dixie reached over the stroller, puckering her lips.

"Please," the boy said, grabbing her face and kissing her.

God, Kent missed when his Elle was a toddler and so willing to show affection. Now, she sometimes pulled away. Not often, but he could see the writing on the wall.

"I've got some games and stuff on the porch." Elle held her hand out to Nicky. "Can I take him to go play?"

"Sure. Just stay where I can see you and make sure he doesn't put anything in his mouth."

Kent watched as his daughter, who was really growing into a fine young lady, led the little boy up the steps, standing just behind him. She talked to him the entire time like she was the babysitter. His baby girl really wasn't a baby anymore.

But he still couldn't ignore the nerves settling in his gut about leaving Elle with this young woman. It reminded him of the first day he'd sent Elle off to school on the bus. Jackie had to force him not to follow it to school.

"I appreciate you filling in today, but I was just about to see if someone could cover my shift." He mentally kicked himself for being so curt. "I'm sure you have other things to do, and your husband…" He knew she didn't have one, so why did he go there?

"I'm not married." She held up her hand, wiggling her fingers. "And until my aunt gets back, I don't have a sitter to go look for a job, so please don't take the time off just because you think you're putting me out. You're not. I could use the money, honestly."

Jackie had spoken about her niece with the adorable boy who had a deadbeat for a dad. Something about constantly being late with child support and recently taking off without a word. What a jerk.

Yeah, Kent didn't need this drama in his life.

He second-guessed Dixie's ability to handle his darling, well-behaved daughter and her seemingly rambunctious toddler. He glanced over at Elle. She certainly had it under control, but he wasn't about to let it go. He couldn't and he had no idea why. "It's for the best if I stay home."

"Why would you do that?"

"My daughter, your son." He raised his palms to the sky. "It's a lot for one person to handle."

"She's ten, and from what Jackie tells me, an angel. And I've been taking care of my son since before he was born. I think I can handle it."

"I've never left my daughter with anyone but my mother and Jackie."

"Seriously?" She adjusted her ponytail, tugging at her blond hair, which bounced over her shoulders. "You've never used a babysitter? What about playdates when she was younger?"

"No to the babysitter and playdates were always

at my house or Jackie was with her." He glanced over his shoulder. Elle had Nicky on her lap as she read him a book. Kent was not ready for his buttercup to no longer need constant supervision. His mother had told him the last time she'd come to visit that he hovered too much and that her walking the few blocks to the park alone would be just fine. The only way to let her spread her wings and find herself was to give her some freedom.

Freedom knocked up a girl he barely knew, making him a dad at twenty. Of course, he had no regrets other than Elle's mother's passing. He hadn't loved Eleanor, something he still felt residual guilt over to this day. They dated for about four months before calling it off. She had trouble with him being in the military, and he didn't care enough to fight for the relationship.

Then she came to him a few weeks after they'd broken up and informed him he was about to be a father. He never once questioned her decision to keep the baby and promised he'd be there every step of the way. They even tried getting back together, but the best they could do would be to co-parent. Only, Eleanor had developed an infection right after giving birth and died two days later, leaving him to raise their daughter alone.

"I'm sorry you came out here, but this doesn't feel right." Jesus, what the fuck was wrong with him? He didn't even have a solid experience with this insanity. Elle was perfectly content. The little boy seemed easy enough.

He'd finally lost it.

Dixie cocked her head, glaring at him as if her eyes were machine guns pelting bullets through the air. "First, I walked what, six blocks? And second. Doesn't feel right? I'm Jackie's niece, and she wouldn't recommend me to you if she didn't trust me."

He arched a brow. "She's my little girl. I don't just trust her with anyone, willy-nilly."

"Never said you did, and as a mom, I totally understand. I have always had a hard time leaving Nicky, but really—and I mean no offense—you need to lighten up."

"Now you sound like my mother," he mumbled.

"Not your mother, but *a* mother." She let out a long sigh. "Do you have my cell?"

He shook his head, glancing at his watch. He needed to get to work, if he was going to go, though he still held out some hope that he'd be able to weasel his way into a day at home.

With his buttercup.

"Aunt Jackie gave me your number. I'll text you so that you'll have mine, and you can text me or call at any time during the day and check in." She pulled her phone and tapped away with her pretty little fingers. He'd never thought that part of the hand was attractive, or a turn-on, unless they were gripping… Nope, he wasn't going there. Not when it was his babysitter.

Or with small children around.

He honestly didn't know how single parents dated. The few times he'd had sex, as in maybe five or six times a year since his daughter had been born, had been when he'd been pulled away on a special assignment, but one-night stands just weren't his thing.

"There. Just sent it to you."

His phone buzzed in his back pocket, sending a tingle to places a nanny shouldn't have any control over. He pulled out his cell and stared at the number flashing in his text messages.

"Here." She took the phone from his fumbling hands.

He'd never been rendered useless around a woman before. He tried to tell himself he was just off-kilter because this young woman was stubborn. She wasn't going to take no for an answer.

She stared at him for a long moment. "Does your daughter have a smartphone?"

He nodded.

"Considering how uptight you are, I'm assuming you track her phone. If not, I can give access to track mine."

"I don't know," he said.

She reached out, curling her soft fingers around his biceps. "We'll be fine, and if there is a problem, I'll call you."

"I'm only working a day shift for a buddy. But if we get dispatched, I won't be able to answer. Let me give you the number of my buddy's wife." He took his phone and quickly sent her the contact information for Tilly Jordan and Maren Knight. "Both have kids. Maren helps run a marina not far from here, so she might be more accessible than Tilly if you can't reach me."

"You've never left your daughter with your friends' wives?"

He thought about that for a moment. "A few times, but they aren't babysitters, they're moms… yeah. I get where you're going with that one." He waggled his finger. "Point taken."

"Good, now is there anything I need to know? Allergies? Foods you don't want her to have?

Medications? Is there a park nearby that we can walk to?"

He held up his hand. "I wrote a list of things. It's on the kitchen table. She's just learning how to use the stove, but she needs supervision, and I'm sure she'll want to make mac & cheese, especially if Nicky is allowed to eat it."

"Nicky will eat anything you put in front of him, including a mud pie."

"I ate a few of those when I was a little boy." He dug into his pocket and handed her a set of keys. "These are to the house and my car, if you need it, but I'd rather you didn't take my daughter—"

"Stop worrying." She took the key ring, dropping it into her purse. "I don't have a car seat for Nicky, so we won't go anywhere if we can't walk there." She pointed toward his SUV. "How are you getting to work?"

He couldn't help the smile that spread across his face. "I'll show you." He held out his hand. "But I need the keys to my car to get the garage door opener."

She retrieved them, setting them in his palm.

He curled his fingers before she had a chance to pull away. The soft skin of her palm sent a shock wave through his body. "Sorry," he mumbled, releasing her hand. Quickly, he turned, clicking the button and opening his SUV. Reaching inside the driver's door, he tapped the black object hanging from the visor. The garage door rattled, opening slowly, revealing his dark-blue Harley. The Florida sun hit the gas tank, making it shine bright.

Taking her out never got old.

"Wow," she said, stepping into the garage, running her fingers over the leather seat. "This is a limited anniversary edition."

"You know your bikes."

"I grew up on the back of one. My dad loved his Harley."

"He still ride?"

She shook her head. "He was killed in action when I was sixteen."

His heart clenched. One of his biggest fears was leaving his daughter alone in this world. One of the reasons he left the military. But service was in his blood. His father had been a SEAL, and he'd seen some serious action. No matter the danger, the world needed men and women like his father—like her father.

"I'm sorry," he said softly.

"Nicky was named after my dad. I just wish he could have met his grandson." She peered around the corner at the porch. "Nicky never sits still that long unless it's on the front of a motorcycle."

"So you have a motorcycle?" he asked.

"I wish but I can barely afford my car. My dad's Navy buddies show up every once in a while and take me and Nicky out on theirs."

"I've got a ton of kid helmets. When I get back from work, I'd happily take him for a ride." He told himself he was only offering to make a little boy happy.

"I don't know. I don't think I can trust you with my kid," she said with a smirk and an arched brow.

"Again, point taken," he said. "Buttercup, Dad's leaving. Come give me a hug and a kiss."

"Stop calling me that," Elle said. "It's so embarrassing."

He laughed, pushing his bike onto the driveway.

"Mommy! I want a ride!" Nicky held on to the railing with one hand and Elle's hand with the other as his tiny little legs navigated the lopsided steps.

"Sorry, buddy. Mr. Carter has to go to work." Dixie scooped up her kid, smacking her lips against his cheek as he scrunched his face, wiggling his body, trying to get down. "And if we don't kick his butt to the curb now, he'll never leave."

That caught a chuckle from Elle. "Don't give him a reason to stay. He's weird that way."

"But, Mommy, I want to go now," Nicky wailed.

"When I get back, little man. Deal?" Kent held out his fist.

Nicky immediately clenched his hand and pounded Kent. "Deal."

"Bye, Dad." Elle wrapped her arms around his middle.

He tugged her close as he kissed the top of her head, holding on for as long as she'd let him. "I love you."

"I love you, too," she said, backing away. "And please don't call and text me twenty times. We'll be fine."

"He seriously does that?" Dixie asked.

"I would never." He kicked his leg over the seat. One of the reasons he'd bought this particular luxury bike over a roadster had been the backrest for him and a safer back seat for his daughter. "But I'm still going to try to get someone to cover my shift."

"Suit yourself." Dixie turned on a dime, her son on her hip, taking Elle by the hand. "I thought my aunt was kidding when she said your dad was over-protective, but he's like from another planet."

"I heard that," he said before turning over the engine and revving it for effect. "It only makes me want to come home sooner."

But he wasn't sure if it was because he was that concerned or he liked the banter.

Or both.

3

Dixie settled on a bench in the neighborhood park just three blocks away from the sexy firefighter's home. Kent exemplified pure, raw human sexuality at its finest. His dark hair, while cut short, still showed off thick, soft waves. His eyes, the color of the best bottle of bourbon, cast a sense of honor wherever his gaze landed. His body, the way it filled out his dark T-shirt and loose-fitting jeans, was more like a temple needing to be worshipped.

Her breath had gotten stuck in her throat when she'd touched his arm, feeling his thick muscles twitch.

When he'd rode off down the street on his Harley, she'd clutched her chest and let out an audible sigh that didn't go unnoticed by her son or Elle.

She pushed the vision from her head and waved to her son as he pumped his chubby little legs back and forth on the swing.

Elle pushed Nicky, all the while talking to him, and he smiled like he hadn't a care in the world, as it should be for a three-year-old. But their life was anything but easy.

She was going to have to split whatever Kent paid her with Elle because she did more work playing with Nicky than Dixie had taking care of Elle. Of course, Elle was quite mature for a ten-year-old and smart, too. She'd rattled off all sorts of information during lunch about the area and its wildlife. She was a little walking encyclopedia. Full of life and laughter.

"Watch, Mommy!" Nicky jumped off the swing, and Elle did her best to prevent him from falling.

"That's great!" She clapped enthusiastically, fighting the tears that came with loving her little boy so much, but not being able to care for him in the way he deserved. She needed to do better by him. "Elle is teaching you a lot of things today."

"I love Elle! She's so much fun." Nicky ran to the slide, Elle tagging along right behind him. A dozen or so other children ran around the park or hung from the jungle gym, and a couple had settled in the sandbox. A group of women, who could be mothers or nannies, gathered under a big tree, chatting, occasionally looking in her direction. A few of them had said hello to Elle but didn't bother with more than a nod to Dixie.

That was fine by her. She had a job to find. No way would she stay at her aunt's house for more than a month. It had been hard enough to tell her she'd been evicted from her trailer and that Nicky's deadbeat father, Daniel, had taken off and hadn't paid child support in over six months. Without that money, she couldn't afford daycare and her rent, let alone make sure Nicky was properly fed.

Shame heated her cheeks. Her father would have been so disappointed in how her life had turned out. Pushing the negative thoughts away, she focused her attention on her iPad and finding a job. She immediately scanned the secretarial section. She stayed away from any listing regarding social work. She'd only had one year of college with the intention of majoring in social services, but that dream died when she could no longer manage working, paying a babysitter, and going to school, especially when Daniel didn't do his share when it came to Nicky.

Glancing over her tablet, she eyed Elle and Nicky, now settling into the sandbox with a little girl who looked about Nicky's age and seemed to know Elle. Dixie had to give props to Elle for being so attentive with Nicky when there were a couple other girls her age at the park who had bugged her to go play with them a few times. Dixie offered Elle every opportunity to dump Nicky back to her, but Elle said she'd prefer to play with him, even stating that her father would expect her to a good little helper.

A tall, slender woman with long blond hair, pushing a high-end baby stroller, handed the little girl in the sandbox a few buckets and shovels, telling her to make sure she shared with the other children. This woman wore a pair of red Bermuda shorts and a white short-sleeved shirt that appeared to be designer. Not that Dixie had any contact with expensive clothing, but this lady's outfit looked pricey.

Glancing around, she noted that most everyone in the park dressed better than she had with old jean shorts that had been out of style for years. She bought her shirt in a secondhand store when she'd been shopping for new-used clothes for Nicky. One day, hopefully soon, she'd be able to spend a few extra dollars and get something special for him. Something brand new, meant just for him, no one else. Every little boy deserved at least one thing like that.

Dixie went back to the four jobs that looked appealing, but she hadn't the qualifications for any of them, even though she knew without a doubt she'd be able to perform them as well as anyone else. She understood computers and knew how to use all the major software programs, and what she didn't know, she'd be able to pick up quickly. All she had to do was get one of these people to take a chance on her, and she'd prove they'd made the right decision.

"Hello." The graceful woman from the sandbox made her way across the park, as the stroller she pushed bumped uneasily over the grass. "I'm Tilly."

"Nice to meet you. I'm Dixie." She pushed to the side of the bench, making room. She didn't feel like being social, but her father and grandmother, rest their souls, taught her to be polite and kind. No reason to hog the seating.

Tilly looked to be about thirty to thirty-five, at best guess. A few wrinkles had started to develop around her eyes, but other than that, her skin looked radiant with the way the sun hit her face. "I don't mean to be rude, but my son doesn't always share well, and I'm not sure the young lady—"

"Elle is perfectly capable of caring for both children while we watch from a safe distance, despite what her father says." Tilly lifted the flap of the stroller where a plump baby, of maybe a year old, slept peacefully.

"You know Kent?"

"My husband works as a firefighter with him and they served in the Air Force together. They've been friends for over ten years."

"Oh, you're the Tilly he gave me contact information for," Dixie said, biting back a smile. "I've never seen a man so overprotective before. He almost didn't want to leave Elle with me. It was the strangest thing, though I probably shouldn't have said that."

"You're not telling me anything I don't already know and the idiot asked me to come check on you." Tilly shook her head. "Kent is a great guy and an even better father, but he's the biggest worrywart I've ever met for a macho fireman."

That might be true, but she was a perfect stranger to Kent and his daughter. Lots of parents these days used nanny cams and other devices to make sure their children were getting the best possible care. It really didn't matter that her aunt Jackie had been Elle's nanny since Elle had been eight weeks old. She loved that child so much that when Kent left the Air Force and moved to Jacksonville, Jackie moved too. She would never intentionally put Elle in danger, which included recommending a replacement while she had to be away, but she could understand Kent's reservations. As a parent, Dixie would have the same ones.

"I've texted him my every move," Dixie said, glancing at the sandbox, her heart swelling at the vision of her son playing nice. He was a good boy, but being an only child, he often struggled with sharing. It didn't help that his father was in and out of his life, confusing the poor boy.

"He wanted me to just watch you, but no way would I do that, plus my daughter would have run to Elle, and I didn't want to put her or Elle in a tough situation, so I thought I'd just come introduce myself."

"Thanks. I appreciate the honesty," Dixie said, tucking her iPad in her purse. She'd have time to send in her resumes this evening, after she proofed them one last time. "Do you live around here?"

God, she hoped so. She'd feel bad if Tilly had to drive any distance with two small children to spy on her.

"We live closer to the marina in Whispering Hills."

"Nice area." Dixie had driven through the neighborhood, admiring the larger homes with their fancy landscaping and perfectly lined palm trees. The homes weren't overtly pretentious, but they were expensive compared to where Kent lived, which was a good neighborhood with nice people, but the cost of housing was substantially less.

Her aunt had been trying to get her to move to the area for a year, telling her to stop trying to force her ex to have a decent relationship with their son. Part of Dixie wanted her son to have the family she hadn't, with two parents who worked together to raise their children. The other part knew Daniel would never step up to the plate and be a real father.

"We like it there. It's close to work for Rex, and I have a home office over the garage." Tilly spoke with a certain grace to her voice. The way she pronounced each syllable gave way to not only style, but intelligence, and not in a way that put anyone off.

"What do you do? If you don't mind me asking." Dixie craved adult conversation more than she realized. For the last few months, she'd worked double shifts and what few hours of free time she had, she'd spent every second with her son. Her throat closed with guilt. For the majority of her life, she'd lived with her dad, only visiting her mother occasionally, who was a free spirit and couldn't settle into being a mother full-time.

"I run a private foundation and a charity to help battered women and children find safe places. We focus on education and helping them get on their feet so they don't go back to their abusers."

"Wow. That sounds amazing and stressful." Dixie had volunteered at a shelter when she'd been in high school as part of her service project. All she ever wanted to do was help people, only she never could manage to help herself. One bad decision after the other left her alone and broke. She literally had a hundred dollars to her name.

"It's both, but I've got an amazing team and one hell of a husband."

An alien ringtone echoed from inside Tilly's purse, and she jumped. "Oh my God. I hate that sound. My husband is constantly changing my ringer, thinking it's just hilarious." She dug into her bag and pulled out a cell. "I'm sorry, I've got to take this." Tilly stood, taking a few steps away from the bench.

Dixie's gaze went between her son and the little boy stretching in the stroller. Life here seemed so much easier in this seaside town. Peaceful. Something she hadn't felt since before her father died. Since that day, her life was a constant, uphill battle where just as she was about to climb to the top, something shoved her down, sending her rolling out of control.

"Sorry about that. One of the hazards of being the boss is I never really get a day off," Tilly said, tossing her phone into the bag before bending over and resting her hand on the baby's tummy. "This little fellow sleeps more than Annabelle has in her entire life."

"How old is he?"

"He will be a year next week. We're having a birthday party. You should come and bring your son. Looks like he and Annabelle have hit it off." Tilly pointed across the park to where Annabelle had wrapped her arms around Nicky.

"I'm shocked he hasn't pushed her away. He can be a little devil sometimes." Dixie watched in amazement as Nicky hugged the cute little girl with curly blond locks like her mother.

"I wish we could stay longer and let the kids play, but I've got to get back to my office. My assistant is moving in a couple of weeks, and I haven't found a replacement yet, so I need to meet with a couple potential applicants."

Dixie sat up straighter. Her heartbeat increased over the idea she'd even ask this stranger for an opportunity to interview for the job. It would be too forward, but maybe she could ease into it with a few questions. "What does your assistant do, exactly?"

"There is a lot of office work, but also helping me create new programs, assessing current ones, and making recommendations to improve them."

"Sounds interesting." Dixie sucked in a deep breath, letting it out slowly. "Does it require a college degree?"

"Not necessarily. It all depends on the applicant. Their experiences, both professionally and personally. I also take into account whether or not I like them." Tilly tilted her head. "Why? Do you know someone or are you looking for a job?"

"Watching Elle is temporary and after that, I need to find something and I don't want to wait tables," Dixie admitted with butterflies in her stomach. "But I'm not sure I have the kind of experience you're looking for."

Tilly held out a small business card. "Send me your resume but focus on any volunteer work you might have done. Also, include any education/course work you've had. I don't care about the degree, but knowing what you've taken helps me see your interests. My assistant would spend a fair amount of time with me visiting shelters, talking with the very people I'm trying to help. And on the flip side of that, we also do various charity events seeking financial support for our programs."

This had to be too good to be true. Dixie swallowed. "I'll get it to you by morning."

"Great. I'll look it over and set up an interview. I can't promise anything. I've already got five applicants, but I can guarantee you that you will be given a fair shake."

"I appreciate the chance."

"My pleasure." Tilly stepped behind the stroller. "I'm glad I came out here today. I look forward to reading your resume, and I hope to see you at my son's birthday party this weekend. I'll send you the information regarding the party when I get your resume. Or get it from Kent."

"I wouldn't want to impose." Dixie rose,

collecting her things, and walked with Tilly back to the sandbox. She wanted friends, and friends for her son, but she didn't think it would be smart to become too friendly with a potential boss.

"You're not." Tilly scooped up Annabelle, who protested wildly, wanting to stay and play longer. "I'm going to insist you come."

Nicky joined right in, standing up and dancing in circles, flapping his little arms.

"Someone is tired," Dixie said.

"Mommy!" Nicky wailed.

She bent down, holding her son by the shoulders. "I see you met a new friend."

"I want to play more," Nicky said, wiping his tired eyes.

"How about we set up a playdate?" Tilly said, holding Annabelle, while the child squirmed. "Would you like that?"

"Yessssss!" Annabelle waved.

"When you come to the interview, bring him. I have a babysitter for when I'm working, so they can play. No problem," Tilly said. "Trust me. I understand how hard it is to find quality sitters." She winked. "Besides, Kent did mention that you're a single mother."

"I see." Dixie never liked her personal business

being discussed behind her back, but she'd give Kent a pass on this one. It's not like she wouldn't have given up that information anyway. "I'm babysitting Elle all this week, except Wednesday."

"Great. I'll make sure we set it up for Wednesday," Tilly said.

"Oh, goodie. A day at Uncle Rex's house," Elle said, kneeling next to Nicky. "He's got a pool!"

"Elle, you just gave me a great idea," Tilly said, tucking Annabelle into the stroller. "I know the team has a day off in two days before doing an overnight rotation. I think you, your dad, and Dixie and Nicky should come over for dinner. We can do the interview and have a nice barbeque."

"Oh no. Really. That would be too much." Dixie could deal with bringing her son on an interview where a babysitter was provided, but no way would she do dinner and a birthday party. Hell, she wasn't going to do either and not just because she wanted to keep Tilly at a safe distance just in case she got the job, but she wouldn't last five minutes in the same room with Kent and not act like a teenage groupie.

"It will be fun. Let's say we all meet at my house around two, and we'll do hamburgers and hot dogs on the grill around five."

"I really—"

"I'm not going to take no for an answer." Tilly waved her hand in the air dismissively before pushing the stroller. "I have a good feeling about you, Dixie."

"Looks like you're going to dinner," Elle said, taking her hand. "Uncle Rex says Aunt Tilly is a force to be reckoned with and whatever she wants, she gets."

"I bet your uncle is dead right on that one." Dixie kissed Nicky on the forehead as he nuzzled his face in her neck, breathing deeply, moments away from a long overdue nap. While he napped, she'd make something for supper and find the perfect excuse not to go to Tilly's, but after she had the interview… no, that would be rude.

Damn, she was going to dinner.

Kent sat at the kitchen table in the fire station and stared at the text from Tilly.

Tilly: *You're nuts. Dixie is great and Elle is going to be a fine little babysitter NEXT YEAR. You're a fool if you can't see that.*

He sighed.

He wasn't ready for any of this. When he became a single father at twenty, no one told him that his little bundle of joy would someday grow up and become a young lady. He wished for the days when his biggest worry was if she'd fall the down the stairs. Those days were easy.

Fuck. Who was he kidding. Nothing was easy about being a dad.

"I can't believe you sent my wife to check on the hot babysitter." Rex slapped him on the shoulder. He plopped himself in the chair across from Kent and glared. "What the hell were you thinking?"

"He did what?" Hawke yelled from his perch in the common room.

"No children, no opinion." Kent set his phone on the table and lifted his soda, chugging half of it. "And you." He waggled his finger at Rex. "Are you really going to sit there and tell me you've never been concerned about a sitter before?"

"It's Jackie's niece, for fuck's sake. We've all known Jackie forever and all the woman has ever done is talk about her brother's darling daughter."

"Who's been through some shit." Kent cocked his head. "And she's got a rambunctious toddler to look after."

Rex smacked his forehead. "Do you even hear yourself?"

"Yeah. I do," Kent admitted. "I can't help myself. Elle's my world. I've only left her with Jackie and my mom."

"Look. I get it. I do. But you take it to insane levels. In a couple of years, Elle's not going to need a nanny. She'll be at the age where she can get off the bus and be home alone." Rex tapped his fingers on the table. "And you're going to have to let her whether you're ready or not. You can't keep stifling the poor child. Not if you want her to grow up and be self-reliant."

"She's ten, not twenty-one."

Rex laughed. "If you want her to learn how to take care of herself, she's going to have to spread her wings. She needs to fall down a few times. Make mistakes. Screw up and that all starts now. You're a great father. The best. But you're smothering her and she's going to rebel in the worst way if you don't start loosening the reins."

Kent glanced over his shoulder as Garth strolled into the room and nodded. Kent glanced at his watch. Finally, time for him to go home. He stood. "You're the one who tells everyone that you're never going to allow Annabelle to date."

Rex winced. "Yeah, that does weird me out, but only because she's exactly like her mother. Aggressive. She's already told me she's marrying little Tommy next door. But after today, it might be Nicky. Tilly sent me this picture." He pulled out his cell and turned it, showing off a picture of Annabelle with her arms around Nicky in a death grip. Her lips were firmly planted on his cheek.

"Oh my God. That's too cute." Kent held the phone in one hand, his other tapping the center of his chest. Elle stood in the background, smiling proudly. "Annabelle has always been a forward little girl."

"Not something a father needs to be reminded of." Rex took his cell. "But my point is I'm doing my best not to destroy that little girl's personality. She's going to grow up on me and it's my job to teach her how to get along in this world."

"And to protect her."

"No shit," Rex said. "But you're trying to shelter Elle from everything. You can't keep doing that. She needs to experience some things that will teach her how to get along without you."

Kent appreciated his friend's words. He knew they were true, but he didn't know how to live them. The last ten years of his life had been centered around making sure Elle had a normal life. Or as normal as a single father could give her. Letting go, even a little, pained his heart. "I worked my entire shift and the worst thing I did was have Tilly check on them."

"Not exactly what you did, but if that helps you sleep at night, you can have it your way," Rex said. "Just remember you and Elle are never alone in this."

"Thanks, man." Kent took his empty soda can and tossed it in the recycle bin. "I'll see you tomorrow." He headed out the door and toward his Harley. He climbed on and turned the key. The sun had begun its decent behind the horizon, casting a fiery glow in the sky. This was one of his favorite times to ride. He revved the engine and peeled out of the parking lot.

The ride home would take about fifteen minutes and he would enjoy every second. Normally, he would savor this time, using it to clear his thoughts from the day so he could be completely present for his daughter. Only tonight, all he could think about was Dixie. Her son. And had Elle gotten the attention she needed.

Mentally, he groaned.

Rex made some valid points. Elle wasn't a baby

anymore. She was at an age where while Daddy was still her hero, she didn't always want to be with him. She wanted to do things on her own.

Like walk to the park.

Or help out a neighbor all by herself.

She was pushing boundaries, and he didn't think she was ready for that kind of responsibility. However, all of his buddies thought differently.

He pulled into his driveway with his thoughts all jumbled. The front door opened and Elle emerged holding Nicky on her hip.

That image sucker punched his good senses.

His little girl looked so grown-up.

"Hey, Daddy." Elle waved.

He climbed off his Harley and strolled toward the steps. "How was your day?"

Nicky rested his head on Elle's shoulder, gripping her shirt.

"It was fun," she said. "Look, Nicky. It's my dad." She patted the little boy's back. She really did have a way with small children.

"Hey, little man." He reached out to ruffle the kid's hair, but he turned his head and practically tried to climb over Elle's shoulder.

Kent recoiled his hand.

"Dixie said he's kind of shy around men." Elle

readjusted Nicky. "It's okay. My daddy's really nice. He doesn't bite or anything."

Nicky turned his head. "You came home, just like you promised." His lower lip quivered as if he might start bawling any minute.

"I try not to make promises I can't keep," he said with his heart in his throat. "Where's Dixie?"

"In the kitchen making dinner."

Nicky pointed to the motorcycle. "Ride!"

"Let me go make sure it's okay with your mom first." He squeezed Elle's forearm, being careful not to touch Nicky. Whatever his issues were with men, he didn't want to add to them. "Are you okay out here with him for a few minutes?"

"Dad, really?" Elle glared, rolling her eyes, before sitting on the floor near a set of blocks.

Nicky folded his pudgy little legs, grabbing one. He glanced up. "You come home every day?"

"Sometimes he has to stay over at the fire station or he's called on a special assignment with the Aegis Network, but most nights he's home." Elle lined up a few more blocks in front of Nicky.

Kent closed his eyes for the count of five before blinking them open. His heart broke in a million pieces. "Make sure he doesn't dart off into the street."

"Oh my God, Dad. I'm not stupid."

"Don't get fresh with me, young lady." He lowered his chin. "And don't use that word in front of him again."

"Yes, Daddy."

Kent opened the door and made his way through the family room and into the kitchen, where the smell of pasta and sauce assaulted his senses.

Dixie sat at the table in front of her iPad. She glanced up. "Oh, hello."

"You didn't have to make dinner," he said.

She tucked her device into a small pouch. "I figured after a long day at work, the last thing you wanted to do was cook." She rose, pointing to the oven. "It's nothing special. Just my aunt's spaghetti pie recipe. There's enough for leftovers, so you can take some for lunch tomorrow."

"What are you and Nicky going to do for dinner?"

"We'll find something at my aunt's house."

"That's just silly," he said. "You went to all this trouble. You might as well enjoy it. Besides, I told Nicky I'd take him for a ride when I got home and while I'm not sure he trusts me, he did point to my bike and said *ride.*"

"I'm sure he'd love it, but I don't want to put you out."

"You're not. The only question is, should I do it now or after dinner?"

"It won't be ready for another twenty minutes," she said.

"All right. Let's go find a helmet that fits him." He waved his hand toward the porch. "After you." He followed her through the house, trying desperately not to watch her hips sway back and forth, but it proved impossible.

Her beauty was undeniable.

She carried herself with confidence, but there was pain etched in her soulful eyes. He knew that look and it gave him pause.

"Mommy!" Nicky jumped to his face and raced to his mother. "He came back!" He wiggled his fingers, begging for his mom to pick him. "Ride! Ride! Ride!"

"Yes, my little lovebug. You can go for ride. But you have to promise you will sit still and do whatever Kent tells you. Got it?"

Nicky grabbed her face and smacked his lips against hers. "Promise."

Kent laughed. He missed those days with Elle. Now he was lucky if she kissed him goodbye at the bus stop. "Come on, little man. Let's go find you a helmet."

"We tried on a few today," Elle said. "We were playing with my old motorized Jeep and since he's a bit of a daredevil, we thought it might be a good idea for him to wear one."

"I like to hear that." He wrapped his arm around Elle, kissing her temple. Thankfully, she didn't pull away.

"I'll go get it." She raced into the garage and reappeared with a helmet.

Kent watched in awe as she helped Nicky strap it on.

"She's so good with him," Dixie said. "Is it okay if I give her a little money? I feel like she did more today than I did."

"That's not necessary. I'm sure Elle loved every second of it. She can't get enough of my friends' kids." Kent held Dixie's gaze.

"Yeah. I noticed that. At the park." She cocked her head. "I should be insulted."

He ignored the statement. "Okay, little man. Are you ready?"

"Yes!"

Kent knelt in front of Nicky. "Can I lift you up on the motorcycle?"

Nicky nodded.

"All right. Let's go." He took Nicky in his arms and placed in front before climbing on the bike. He revved the engine.

The little boy squealed in delight.

They drove around the neighborhood, keeping it slow and safe. This wasn't his kid, so he was going to make sure nothing happened. That thought made him chuckle. He wouldn't dream of letting his little girl ride with just anyone.

When he pulled back into his driveway, it surprised him that neither Elle nor Dixie were waiting for them. He helped Nicky off the bike and took off the helmet. "Come on, little man. Let's go find your mommy." He took Nicky's hand and walked up the steps. The second he opened the door, the boy bolted through the house.

"Mommy! Mommy! Where are you?"

"I'm right here." She knelt at the kitchen threshold with open arms. "Did you have a nice ride?"

Nicky leaped into his mother's arms. "Are we coming here again?"

"Tomorrow," Dixie said.

"Will he come home again?" Dixie rose, hugging her little boy tight. "Yes, baby."

Elle meandered toward Kent. She leaned into him, resting her head against his arm. "We're going to have so much fun tomorrow, I promise."

"I should get going," Dixie said.

"What about dinner?" Kent shouldn't push. He didn't want to strike up a friendship with this woman. She was a temporary babysitter while her aunt was away.

Yet not only did her little boy tug at his heartstrings, but she did something to his soul.

"I hope you don't mind, but I packed some up for us to take home," Dixie said. "Nicky melts down right after dinner and he didn't get in a good nap. He'll be a bear if I don't get him to bed soon."

"I remember those days well."

"Thanks for taking him for a ride. I really appreciate it," she said. "I'll see you tomorrow."

"I heard Tilly invited all of us over to her place on Wednesday."

Dixie blinked. "I'm not sure if we should go. I don't want to intrude."

Kent chuckled. "You'd insult her if you didn't go."

"It will be fun. And Annabelle loves Nicky. Come on. Please?" Elle pleaded.

"I'll think about it." Dixie nodded. "I really

need to go before this one realizes he's going to be missing out on something." She snagged her bag and waltzed right out the door.

Elle glanced up and smiled. "I think Daddy likes someone."

"I think my daughter needs to stop trying to fix me up with every single woman she meets." He arched a brow.

"She checks all the boxes." Elle pulled back a chair at the table and pointed to the plate of food. "She can cook. She's pretty. She's kind, smart, and she didn't think you were too crazy."

He joined his daughter at the table. "For the record, your old man isn't looking for a lady. I've already got one of those in my life and I'm staring at her."

Elle rolled her eyes, like she did about a million times a day. "I'm not going to be around forever to take care of you."

He groaned. No truer words were ever spoken.

4

Kent snagged the beer that Rex offered and took a healthy swig while he watched his daughter do a flip off the diving board, biting his tongue when he wanted to tell her to be careful. Everyone kept telling him he needed to lighten up when it came to Elle. While he knew they were all correct, it was impossible when you were both the mother and father.

Nicky and Annabelle sat in the round plastic kiddie pool, pouring water over his knees and laughing. Nicky certainly wasn't shy when it came to other kids and women, but he did tend to be reserved around men.

That poor boy. To have a father who popped in

and out whenever he felt like it, but not care enough to be a real dad was something Kent couldn't comprehend. It pained him every day that Eleanor only had a few brief moments in her mother's arms. Eleanor had only been nineteen and had her entire life ahead of her. Kent might not have loved her, but he knew no matter what, he would have been the same kind of father he was now. The only difference would be he'd be sharing time with Elle's mother.

"Kisses, Daddy!" Annabelle stood up in the pool, opening and closing her fingers.

Rex bent over and gave her a big kiss. "Hey, Elle, mind coming over and watching these two crazy lovebirds while I talk to Kent?"

"Not at all." Elle climbed out of the pool, wrapping a towel around her waist, which Kent noticed was starting to change. On the way over, Elle had mentioned that one of her friends had gotten her first training bra, and she was thinking she needed one, too. Kent nearly died right there.

But he wasn't so out of touch that he didn't know that reality was right around the corner, along with all the other things that came with becoming a young woman. Tilly and Maren had both offered to help him in those areas. As did Jackie.

But no one could take the place of a mother. Something that Elle would never experience and that pained him in other ways.

He stood, Nicky holding on to his calf, looking up at him with sad blue eyes.

"You want a kiss, too?" Kent asked.

The little boy nodded.

How could Kent refuse? He scooped him up, planting a loud raspberry kiss on his cheek like he used to do when his daughter had been that age. Nicky squirmed and giggled, kicking his little legs. If Kent ever met the boy's father, he'd punch him before he got the chance to say hello.

"Be a good boy for Elle," Kent said.

"I will!"

He set Nicky down and followed Rex to a table near the deep end of the pool. It always amazed Kent how rich Rex and his wife were, yet for the most part, they lived a modest life. They could have a ten-million-dollar home, but instead, they lived in a middle-class neighborhood, drove middle-class cars, and both worked. The only real difference, besides their net worth, was that they put their money where it counted: helping people who didn't have the same luxuries. And Tilly actually made a difference in the world.

"I take it you heard back from Darius." Kent had only met Darius Ford a few times, but he was a good friend of Arthur's and had helped him and Rex with tracking down information about people over the years. Darius was the kind of guy that if you needed someone found, he'd be able to locate them with the snap of his fingers.

"I did." Rex rested his ankle over his knee, tipping back his longneck. "Her ex isn't a very nice boy."

"Boy?"

"Well, he's twenty-three, which is so young to be a father."

"I was twenty when I had Elle, and Dixie's only twenty-three," Kent said, wishing he hadn't sounded so defensive because Nicky's father didn't deserve defending. "Tell me what Darius dug up."

"For starters, he has a record."

Kent glanced over his shoulder. The second Nicky spied him, he waved frantically. Kent smiled, waving back. Damn kid was going to steal his heart.

"Please tell me it wasn't for any kind of abuse," Kent said, turning his attention back to his buddy.

Rex was a few years older, but they had gone through fire training together. Rex had been shocked that Kent had a kid, and Kent had been shocked Rex was loaded. Even more shocked when Tilly walked back into his life and bam, next thing you know, the dude's married with babies.

Lucky man.

"Unlawful entry, larceny, and a few possession charges. He's never done time, only a few nights in county lockup and probation." Rex pushed his sunglasses down and peered over the rims. "His boss at the auto shop said he quit because he got some great new opportunity on the west coast."

Kent tipped his beer, glancing up at the office over the three-car garage where Dixie was interviewing for a job as Tilly's assistant. Good for her. She needed an opportunity like that.

"Do we know where, exactly?" Kent wasn't the kind of guy that wished bad things on other people, even criminals, but he so wished this jerk-off was out of the picture, for good.

Rex shook his head. "His landlord said he didn't pay his last month's rent and just left one morning."

"What the hell did she see in an asshole like that?"

"Not much, according to Darius' sources," Rex said, shoving his glasses back. "She broke up with him before she had Nicky. He claimed the kid wasn't his. She did the whole paternity thing and nailed him for child support."

"Which he's barely ever paid, according to Jackie," Kent muttered. He understood she needed help financially, but if this Daniel guy was going to keep fucking with Nicky's heart, then no amount of money would be worth it.

"She tried taking him to court, but according to the records, she had to bail because she didn't have the money to continue." Rex pushed his phone across the table. "That's where she was living until a few weeks ago. She was evicted when she couldn't pay the rent."

Kent stared at the run-down trailer in a dumpy park. He'd seen worse. Hell, he'd lived in worse.

"She lost her job waiting tables when she could no longer afford daycare."

"Jesus Christ." He'd seen his share of hard times, but he'd always managed.

Jackie had told Kent things were rough for her niece, but she also said that Dixie had been making it work. That she was tough, resourceful, and stubborn. Obviously, she'd lied to her aunt until she couldn't lie anymore. He understood pride.

Respected it. He also respected a person who could ask for help when they truly needed it.

"You know my wife does a background check on everyone she hires, right?"

"She hasn't hired Dixie."

"Yet," Rex said. "But she did the check anyway because she had one of her feelings and you know how Tilly gets when she wants to help someone."

"This is beginning to feel like spying. I just wanted to know what happened to her ex. What kind of man he was since she's babysitting my daughter, and I don't want that kind of crap to touch Elle."

Rex leaned forward and tapped his finger on the table. "Her bad judgment one night doesn't make for a lifetime of poor decisions and just because he's a deadbeat, doesn't mean she's not a decent person."

"I never said that."

"She's a good woman. All three references she gave talked her up as this strong, independent person, with a good work ethic, and a kind heart. Even the landlord who evicted her and the restaurant owner who had to fire her, said they would have given her a second chance had she been able to pay her bills or have regular daycare. They all knew her situation and hated doing what they did, but they had businesses to run."

"Hard to do when you're in that vicious cycle."

"She's just a woman who is down on her luck and needs a break. Tilly sees this all the time, and I would bet the sports car my wife made me sell that she hires Dixie."

"That would certainly help her get on her feet, and I know Jackie plans on babysitting Nicky to help her, but what if this Daniel asshole shows up? That's the last thing she and her son needs."

"This coming from the man who gets his panties in a wad when paternal rights are screwed with." Rex held up his hand. "Let's get to the heart of the matter. You've got the hots for Dixie."

Kent tried to stop the corners of his mouth from curling into a smile but gave up. "That's beside the point. Even if I acted on that, and I won't, I certainly wouldn't feel threatened if her ex showed up, but it would concern me for Elle, which is why I'm not going to pursue her."

"Like hell you're not." Rex shook his head, laughing. "You can't stop looking at her. Man, you're practically drooling."

"I am not," he said, still smiling. Any man with a pulse would notice Dixie. "But she is super sexy."

"Really? You think so? I don't know. I haven't really noticed her or anything."

Kent balled up a napkin and tossed it at Rex. "You're a married man, and Dixie is… she's… well, off-limits."

"To just us married folk? Or any man, other than you?"

Kent sucked in a deep breath, letting it out slowly. "Any man."

———

"Why'd you drop out of college?"

Dixie swallowed the thick lump that had formed the second she'd gotten in Kent's car an hour ago. Between fighting her attraction and wanting this job, her nerves were frazzled to the point she could barely string together a coherent thought. She stared at Tilly and cleared her throat. The interview had gone along well enough thus far. Now it was time to be honest because hiding the truth hadn't been working out too well.

"It was hard enough being a single mother; adding the expense of college, it was just too much."

Tilly leaned back in her large white leather

chair, resting her delicate hands on the armrests. "You wanted to be a social worker?"

"I wanted to do something in social services or maybe women's health."

"It must have been hard for you to give up your dreams."

Dixie shook her head. "Nicky means everything to me. I don't see it as giving up anything when I've gained him."

"I like you," Tilly said, smiling. "Starting salary is forty thousand—"

Dixie went into a coughing fit. No way could she have heard that correctly. The most she'd ever made had been fifteen thousand in one year.

"Are you okay? Do you need some water?"

"No, I'm good. Please continue," Dixie said, mentally preparing herself for a different number.

"As I was saying, the salary is forty thousand. You'll have two weeks paid vacation, five sick days and five personal days. I don't roll them over to the next year. I work from home two days a week and in the office or visiting various programs and shelters the other three, and I expect you to come with me most days. If I need you at an evening function, I usually let you off work early that day or come in later the next day. I have a full-time nanny, if you need her services, but you'd have to work that out with her. My foundation also has a daycare on-site. If you need medical insurance, I can add you, but that comes out of your salary. You can look over the plan and let me know at any time."

Dixie curled her fingers over the hem of her sundress to keep them from shaking. Her heart pounded so loud she thought for sure she wasn't hearing everything right. "Are you offering me the job?"

"It's yours for the taking." Tilly stood, holding out a folder. "The details of the job offer and all the responsibilities are in this packet. Take tonight and read this. You can let me know tomorrow if you want the job or not." She leaned across the desk. "I hope you'll take it."

"Thank you." Her hands trembled slightly as she took the folder. She fought the tears forming in her eyes. "I won't disappoint you."

"Is that an acceptance?"

Dixie nodded.

"Well, all right, then," Tilly said. The way her mouth tipped up into an elegant smile radiated confidence. "Let's go downstairs and celebrate."

Dixie stuffed the papers in her purse and followed Tilly out of the office and down the staircase that led to a back corner in the family room off the kitchen.

"Do you like white wine?" Tilly asked as she reached into a wine cooler.

"I do, thanks." In the matter of three days, she'd landed a job and not just any job. Her aunt was right. This would be a fresh start. Her only worry now was Nicky.

"You look deep in thought." Tilly set two glasses on the white granite counter adorned with green and light-gray swirls. The entire kitchen looked clean. Crisp. It had white and light-green shaker-style cabinets and a whitewashed wood floor.

Laughter filtered through the screen door. Nicky jumped from the side of the pool into Kent's arms, screaming to do it again. Elle hung on her father's back, egging Nicky on. He'd managed being a single parent just fine, which gave her hope. But it pained her how being around him affected Nicky. He craved male attention, and Kent was all male. Elle didn't seem to be as needy around females, but she had Jackie, and from the looks of it, Tilly as well.

"It's been a rough few months, and I'm a little overwhelmed with how quickly things are changing. I'm kind of waiting for the other shoe to drop."

"I'm a good read of people, and I think it's more than that." Tilly pointed to the pool. "Nicky sure is attached to Kent."

"He's usually more guarded with men."

"Why is that?" Tilly asked.

"His father stopped coming around to see him six months ago." The only time Daniel ever really spent time with his son was when she pushed it, a decision she now regretted. "Stopped paying child support nine months ago."

A soft, tender hand rested on her shoulder, sending warmth to her heart.

"Have you tried to find him? Take him to court?"

"I ran out of money and lost the energy." She leaned against the island, sipping the butter-flavored wine, her taste buds exploding with excitement. The wine she'd been used to tasted like ethyl with a mix of berries. Taking a bit more into her mouth, she swirled it around, savoring every drop. "My mother left my dad when I was four, but really, she left me. She's a bit of a free spirit and not cut out to be a nurturing mother. But my dad was so amazing that somehow he managed to make up for the lack of motherly affection. I thought I could do the same for Nicky."

"Where's your mother now?"

"She recently remarried and is living in the Panhandle. I think she's finally settling down."

"Do you feel loved by her?" Tilly asked.

Dixie nodded. "One thing about my mother is that she has never lied to me. She doesn't make promises she knows she won't keep and neither did my dad. I feel like I've been lying to Nicky because I really don't believe his father loves him, much less wants to be in his life."

"You're a good mom, and Nicky will be okay, especially since we're going to have to make sure he marries Annabelle. Look at them."

The two toddlers walked across the concrete patio holding hands. "At the last daycare I had Nicky in, the teacher always told me he didn't play nice with the other children."

Tilly laughed. "My very first nanny quit because Annabelle was too much for her."

"But she's so calm."

"Annabelle? Calm?" Rex said as he stepped through the sliders. "Your son has put a spell on that child because she's normally a holy terror." He waved a baby monitor. "Lucas is awake."

"He'll want milk," Tilly said.

"I'm on it." Rex breezed by, stopping to give his wife a brief kiss.

Dixie turned her attention to the backyard and gasped as Kent placed his hands on the side of the pool, pushing his upper body out of the water, showing off what could only be described as a twelve-pack. The water beaded off his tanned skin, gliding down like condensation on a frosted mug.

"Not too bad to look at," Tilly whispered.

Dixie jumped, startled. "Oh, I wasn't—"

"Oh yes, you were."

"Okay, maybe a little." Every time she could, she stole a glance at Kent. She'd thought she'd been hiding it well, but now that he was shirtless, it would be hard to take her eyes off him.

"I'm told he works out all the time. Rex says it's because he's sexually deprived."

Dixie's cheeks burned as her jaw dropped open. "I doubt that. He's got to have tons of women throwing themselves at him."

"In the almost four years I've known him, he's never had a girlfriend. Rex has known him for about ten years and said he's seen him with two women." Tilly held up two fingers. "Two."

That had to be impossible. Then again, the last time Dixie had sex was over a year ago and before that had been when she'd gotten pregnant. "Maybe he's just really discreet."

"Why don't you go find out?" Tilly raised her glass. "I dare you."

Dixie waggled her finger. "No… no… no. I'm not interested."

"And I'm not blond." Tilly opened the door. "Hey, Kent, can you come here a minute? Dixie needs help with something."

"I can't believe you just did that."

Tilly looked over her shoulder and winked. "I think Elle could use some help with the rug rats."

Dixie pressed her backside against the counter, steadying herself as she heaved in a deep breath, her mind trying to find something, anything, that she could possibly need help with so she didn't look like a complete ass.

"What's up?" Kent inched closer, his muscles flexing with each step.

"Um… Um… I need your keys. I think I left my bag with my bathing suit in the car."

He raised his hand, his finger landing on her shoulder. Holding her breath, she glanced down just as he flicked the string to her suit.

"Oh." Nah. She didn't look like an ass. She looked stupid. "Guess I wore it."

"Guess so," he murmured, his bare toes touching her flip-flops. "Anything else you need help with?"

His dark-mahogany orbs twinkled with a mischievous glint that stole her breath and made her flesh line with goosebumps.

"I think I'm good," she managed to ground out.

He stood so close, her chest heaved into his hard body.

"I think you need to be kissed."

"I… I… don't think so."

His index finger traced her lower lip.

The room spun. Her insides sloshed around like a teenager about to drive a car for the very first time. Her eyelids fluttered closed against her will as he brushed his mouth over hers, drawing her lower lip between his.

Her legs went limp as she leaned into him for support, clutching at his strong shoulders. His warm tongue slid into her mouth, swirling, teasing, tasting.

He cupped her face, gently breaking off the kiss, his thumbs fanning her cheeks. "I have no idea what I'm doing or why I'm doing it."

"That makes two of us." She dropped her hands to her sides, hoping he'd take a step back.

She needed a little breathing room. "We shouldn't have done that."

"Probably not," he muttered.

"I'm trying to get my life back on track and right now that doesn't include—"

He hushed her with his index finger. "We both have other people in our lives who come first. I get it. So, for now, why don't we enjoy a nice dinner with our kids and friends."

5

Kent sat in his kitchen, sipping his coffee while going through his checklist. The only people who had ever taken Elle overnight had been his mother and Jackie. Had he known his nanny would need to be gone, he would have made arrangements for his mother to fly down, or he'd have found a way to change shifts.

He flipped to the second page, crossing out a couple of things that were no longer relevant.

"No, Daddy, toss that thing away." Elle bounced her way into the kitchen from the family room. Her smile had turned to a frown the second she laid eyes on the folder.

"This has emergency numbers if something happens." He tapped his finger on the paper.

Pursing her lips together, she pointed to the fridge. "And the same information is tacked there."

"I don't know why this bothers you so much."

"Because its sooooo embarrassing. Every new school year, you march yourself down to my new teacher and hand them a piece of paper with *instructions* on how to care for me." Elle held up her hands and made air quotes while she simultaneously rolled her eyes. "They are highly trained professionals in the care of children. Like you are dealing with fires."

"That's not the—"

"Dad, I'm not finished." She planted her hands on her hips.

Kent bit his tongue.

"And anytime I go to a friend's house, you have to get on the phone with the parents."

He held up his hand. "Every parent does that."

She shook her head vehemently. "They don't tell you how to make their kid's sandwich, right down to the exact mixture of mayo and mustard I like." She brushed her hair from the sides of her face. "Which, by the way, it's fine to slop it on the bread. I'm not two anymore, and I don't have a cow if it's not the perfect color."

"I'll make sure I add that to the notes," he said,

waffling between frustration over his daughter's sassy attitude as of late and the sinking feeling in the pit of his gut that perhaps she was right.

Ding-dong.

Elle wiggled her finger.

"Young lady," he said, lowering his chin. "Don't take that tone with me."

"I'm sorry, but if you give that folder to Dixie, she'll be as angry as I am."

"I doubt that. Now go get the door for our breakfast guests."

Last night, after dinner at Rex's, he'd dropped Dixie off at Jackie's house, giving her an awkward hug goodbye at the door. The woman turned his brain to mush.

"Good morning," Dixie said as she breezed into the kitchen like the ocean lapping at the shore. "I hear we're having pancakes for breakfast."

He stood, holding the folder in his hands. "Do you want some coffee?"

"I do. But I can get it." Stretching her arms up, her shirt lifted from her miniskirt, showing off her taut stomach.

Cartoons blared from the family room, reminding him of all the reasons he shouldn't pursue another kiss.

"Here." He held out the folder. "Just some information about staying with Elle for the night."

He swallowed, watching Dixie eye him over the mug, the steam from the coffee floating up toward her face.

She set the mug down, taking the folder between her fingers.

He kept telling himself he was just being a good parent. Elle was his world, and all he wanted to do was make sure she was well looked after when he couldn't be there. So he went overboard with all the tiny details, like how she liked to have her towels warm when she got out of the shower. Of course, she did that herself these days.

"This is six pages long," Dixie said. "And at the end, you have a little test."

He'd added that this morning.

"You're seriously nervous about leaving Elle with me overnight?"

Kent took a small step back. The glare coming off Dixie's sapphire eyes was more like a raging hurricane than the calming of the ocean.

She shoved the folder with his detailed instructions against his chest.

"I did this for your aunt the first time—"

Dixie poked his chest. "Would you be insulted if

I didn't trust you to take care of Nicky for one night?" She stormed out of his kitchen and into the backyard, slamming the door shut.

"Come on, Dixie." Tossing the papers on the counter, he followed her outside, the morning sun already tipping the temperatures well into the eighties. "I can't help that I'm a detail-oriented person. I make lists. Wouldn't you make me a list for Nicky?"

"No. Actually, I wouldn't." She planted her hands on her hips. "You've spent enough time with him for me to feel comfortable knowing you'd take care of him like you would your own."

"You'd leave instructions if you left Nicky with Elle or say the teenager who lives next to Jackie."

"I'm not a teenager."

"I didn't mean to offend you." He couldn't believe his daughter had been right.

"Well, you did."

"And I'm sorry, but as a single parent, you have to be able to see why I'd be a little skittish."

She laughed, but it wasn't a ha-ha funny noise. More like a *har-har, right, asshole* noise. "The first day I came to babysit, yes. The second day, maybe. But now? Absolutely not." She folded her arms. "I'm good enough to kiss, but not good enough to make sure your daughter is safe for twenty-four hours."

He wondered if they'd ever get to the topic of their one kiss yesterday in Rex's kitchen. He knew Tilly was up to her tricks, trying to push them together. The idea to kiss her hadn't appeared in his mind until he stepped into the room, and she looked so sweet and sexy with her concerned expression. He loved the way her nose crinkled, and her right eyelid twitched when she was nervous.

"Dad, we're hungry," Elle said, standing in the doorway with Nicky on her hip.

"Give us ten minutes."

"Fine," Elle said, rolling her eyes before turning and disappearing back into the house.

He swallowed. "Now that is scary," he whispered.

"What is?"

"My daughter with a kid on her hip."

Dixie patted his shoulder. "She's going to grow up someday and fall in love with a man and—"

"Don't say it. Or might I remind you of your little man one day falling in love with a girl and… and… and…"

"Having sex." She no longer shot daggers at him, but now her baby blues doused him with sarcasm.

"And you don't have a problem with that?"

"What, that my son is going to grow up to be a man, and hopefully a good one, like you and not his fath…" She snapped her head toward the house. "Thank God he wasn't standing there."

"I don't think he heard you." He rested his hands on her forearms, gently rubbing up and down. "Your aunt told me his father hasn't been paying child support." He racked his brain for the details of that conversation so as not to muck it up with what Darius had found out. He figured one mistake today was enough.

"He never wanted to be a dad. I kept thinking that as soon as I gave birth, he'd fall in love with his boy, but Daniel just looked at him and told me I needed to prove Nicky was his kid." A tear rolled down her cheek. "How could anyone not love their own child?" She pointed to the house. "Nicky still asks when his daddy is coming back."

"What do you tell him?"

She slumped her shoulders. "I just smile and tell him that his father thinks of him every day."

He bit down on his anger and choked on sadness. "Nicky is a smart kid; that won't work much longer."

"I know. But how do you tell a kid his father doesn't want him?"

"I wish I had an answer." What Kent really wished for was five minutes alone with that weasel. He tipped her chin with his thumb and index finger. "Nicky will grow up to be a fine man because he has you for a mom." He searched her eyes for a reason to pull away. Yesterday, he'd told himself that they would never share another kiss. Things were too complicated, and they both had children to protect.

"Thank you for staying that."

"It's the truth." Cupping the back of her neck, he drew her closer. The bitter smell of roasted coffee flowed from her lips.

"Your neighbor is staring at us."

"Is it Jessica?"

"Yes."

"Good, let's give her something to gossip about at the park today." Before Dixie could protest, he circled his free hand around her waist, crushing her chest to his, and molded his mouth on her lips.

She fisted his shirt as if she were going to shove him away, but instead she relaxed into his arms, resting her soft palms on his shoulder blades. Everything about her excited his body and his mind. He wanted to explore every inch of her skin and listen to her talk until the wee hours of the morning.

The revving of a motorcycle engine reminded him he had to leave for work, and he'd promised to have breakfast with his daughter.

"I don't know about you, but I'm starving," he said, kissing the side of her neck.

"We should go inside. I think Jessica just snapped our picture."

He glanced over his shoulder, then smiled and waved at his nosy, but harmless neighbor. "Beautiful morning, isn't it." Draping his arm over Dixie's shoulders, he guided her to the back door, leaving Jessica with her jaw wide open. "You might want to stay clear of the park today, unless you want to field a dozen or so questions about our relationship."

"We don't have one."

"A second kiss puts us near that territory."

"No, it doesn't," she said, though her smile said something else.

"We'll talk about it when I get back from work."

He opened the door, and Nicky came running… to him.

"Kent!" the little boy wailed. "Don't leave!"

He glanced from Nicky to Dixie, who stared at him with wide eyes. His heart raced as he bent over, lifting the toddler and cradling him in his arms. "What's gotten into him?" he asked his daughter.

"I don't know. I just said you would be gone all night. I didn't know it would upset him. I'm sorry." Elle chomped down on her fingernail.

"It's okay," Dixie said, patting the boy's back. "You had no idea he'd react this way. Come here." She tried to pull him, but he wouldn't let go of Kent's neck.

"Why don't you two start breakfast while Nicky and I go have a man-to-man."

Dixie shook her head, her hands still tugging at her son. He understood her concern, but Nicky had a death grip, and he figured if he didn't handle it, Nicky would make the assumption this was just another man who was going to walk out of his life.

Well, Kent wasn't going to do that.

"We'll just be in the family room." He leaned over and gave her a quick peck on the cheek, which caused his daughter to gasp and then chuckle. He wasn't sure what to make of that, but he was going to have to talk to Elle anyway. He hugged Nicky, rubbing his back, trying to get him to stop sobbing so they could have a little chat, though having real discussions with three-year-olds were generally not too deep.

"Nicky? Do you know what I do for work?" Kent asked.

"No," he said with a quiver in his voice.

"I'm a firefighter."

"Really?" Nicky snapped his head up as Kent sat down on the sofa. "You ride in a red truck?"

Kent laughed. "I do, and you see, if I don't go to work and someone has a fire, who will be there to put it out?"

"But why all-night work?"

"It's just the way we do it sometimes. I'll be home tomorrow morning, and if it's okay with your mom, maybe we can go fishing."

Nicky nodded his head wildly as he wiped his own tears away. "I don't want you to go away like my daddy where he only gets to think about me."

Well, for fuck's sake. Kent did all he could to not punch the wall. This kid deserved better and eventually he'll figure out the truth about his father, but hopefully not until he's ready and mature enough to understand this wasn't his fault.

"How about we go get some pancakes?"

Nicky nodded.

Kent stood and made his way back to the kitchen with a heavy heart. Getting involved with a woman with a deadbeat ex and a toddler was going to be complicated as hell.

"Smells good in here." He handed Nicky to

Dixie, who hugged him like an overprotective mother, which made Kent chuckle. Sitting down at the small round table, he placed a napkin in his lap and a fork in a stack of fluffy pancakes.

"Daddy, wait for the rest of us."

"I've got ten minutes, Buttercup."

Elle put one hand on her hip.

"Fine," he muttered. "Elle, I've got ten minutes before I have to be out the door, so let me stuff my face."

Elle smiled sweetly, setting a couple more plates on the table. Nicky climbed up on his knees, waiting for his pancake.

Once Dixie was seated at the table, Elle patted her father's leg. "A nice, romantic meal, sort of," she said.

He dropped his fork.

Dixie choked on her juice.

Nicky covered his mouth, giggling.

"Come on, Dad. I saw you two kissing out there. And at Uncle Rex's place." She smiled like she just won first prize in the spelling bee. "You're dating."

6

The rich hazelnut scent floated from the dark coffee. Dixie inhaled deeply, letting the aroma fill her lungs, waking her up from what had been a restless sleep. Jackie always did the overnights at her house, but Kent suggested they stay at his based on Nicky's meltdown, and she had to agree.

Only she hadn't anticipated having to smell the combination of fresh palm trees mixed with a hefty dose of pure masculinity all night long while she tried to sleep in his bed. And when she did get a few moments of slumber, her dreams were filled with him climbing between the sheets, caressing her body, and his glorious lips sprinkling sweet kisses all over her skin.

Sipping the scalding dark liquid, she stared out the front window with her feet tucked up under her butt on the sofa. The sun had yet to rise, but the sky had started to lighten from black to a cobalt blue.

"Dixie, I don't feel so good." Elle stood at the opening between the kitchen and the family room, her hand over her stomach.

"Come lie on the sofa with me."

But before Elle could take two steps, her face turned white. "I'm going to be sick," Elle said with wide eyes just before she barfed all over herself.

Dropping the mug to the ground, Dixie raced across the room, knocking over the lamp to get to the gagging child, sidestepping the vomit on the floor. "Let's get you cleaned up." She put her arms around Elle, her nightgown soaked with perspiration.

"I'm sorry," Elle said with a weak voice.

"Don't be sorry. You must have the stomach bug. I hear it's going around."

"My stomach hurts so bad."

Dixie lifted the gown off and rested her hand on Elle's forehead. "You have a fever."

Elle's stomach made a loud gurgling sound as she dropped to her knees, clutching her stomach, throwing up once more, her body shaking as she rolled to her side.

Dixie fumbled for the first aid kit in the linen closet. Kent had mentioned he had those strip things that would take her temperature across her forehead.

Elle moaned on the ground, her pasty body covered in sweat. This was no ordinary stomach bug.

The strip read 104.6.

Fuck.

"I need to get my phone, okay, Elle? I'll be right back." Dixie raced through the house, slipping on the puke twice, but she didn't care. Her hands shook as she quickly shot off a message to Kent, but she knew this needed more. She hit 9-1-1, sitting on the floor next to Elle, cradling her head in her lap.

"9-1-1, what's your emergency?"

"I've got a ten-year-old girl with a fever of 104.6 and she's vomiting and has horrible stomach cramps. It came on while she was sleeping..."

Elle's body convulsed.

Dixie did her best to get the girl to toss her cookies in the trash can.

"She's throwing up nonstop, though it's more dry heaving at this point."

Elle screamed out in pain.

"Is her stomach sore to the touch?" the dispatcher asked.

Dixie rested her shaky hand on Elle's belly, and she cried out again.

"Yes," Dixie said.

"We'll dispatch an ambulance. Stay on the line with me until they arrive, okay?"

"Sure." Dixie gave the woman on the other end the address. She tucked the phone to her ear and lifted Elle into her arms. "Is there any way you can get a message Kent Carter? He's a firefighter. I've got his station number here."

"We can do that," the dispatcher said.

"He's her father."

"I don't want to go to the hospital," Elle said weakly.

"I know, sweetie, but we need to." Dixie held Elle, rocking back and forth on the floor, staring out the window, willing the ambulance to come quicker.

Elle continued to moan, and the 9-1-1 operator continued to talk calmly.

Dixie's insides shook like a collapsing building. She did her best to soothe Elle, but the poor girl was in so much pain. She hadn't eaten much for dinner, but Dixie figured maybe she just didn't like the fish.

Sirens blipped as a police car and an ambulance rolled to a stop in front of the house. Two men jumped from the emergency vehicle, opened the back doors, and pulled out a gurney.

"Ever been in an ambulance before?" Dixie looked down at Elle, her face whiter than pure snow.

"Yes, but just with my dad for fun," Elle said.

"I haven't been in one at all. Looks like we get to do it together." Dixie bent over and kissed Elle's forehead.

"Are you Dixie?" one of the EMTs asked as he stormed through the front door.

"How do you know my name?"

"Kent heard the call come over and reached out to the first responder, which was my station house."

"You know Kent?"

The man nodded. "He's a good man."

"He's on his way?"

"Yes." He bent down and put a stethoscope against Elle's chest. "Could she have gotten into medication? Alcohol?"

"No," Dixie said.

"Could she have eaten anything that could have been bad?"

"We had fish for dinner. She didn't eat much,

but my son and I had the same meal, and we're not sick."

"Does she have any allergies?" the EMT asked.

"She breaks out in hives if she uses cold cream."

"Is she on any medication we should know about?"

"I gave her Tylenol before bed. She complained of a headache." Dixie mentally went through their entire day, trying to think of anything she might have missed.

"Let's get her on the gurney, get an IV drip of fluids started, and transport her to the hospital."

Dixie nodded. "These nice gentlemen are going to put you on that bed and strap you in. I'm going to get Nicky and…" She glanced up as the man scooped up Elle. "I have a three-year-old upstairs. We can both ride with her, right?"

"Sorry, ma'am. You can ride with her, but your son can't."

She stared at the man, tears welling in her eyes. She couldn't leave Elle to ride alone, scared out of her mind. But she didn't have anyone to watch Nicky.

"I can bring him to the hospital," a policeman said. He stood with his thumbs looped in his belt. "If you have a car seat."

"I do. It's in the garage." Thank God she'd remembered to bring it this time just in case. "I'll go get him."

The sound of a Harley roaring at unfathomable speeds rattled her ears.

"Daddy." Elle licked her dry lips.

"He's here." Dixie took Elle's hand as they rolled her out the front door and down the driveway. No way would she let go until Kent was by her side.

Kent skidded his motorcycle to a stop in the driveway. "What happened?" he asked with a harsh bite to his tone.

"Could be food poisoning or maybe appendicitis," the EMT said. "But we won't know until we get her to the hospital."

Kent drew his lips into a harsh line as he curled his fingers around Dixie's wrist. "I'll take it from here," he said, pushing her aside. "Daddy's here, Buttercup. Everything is going to be okay."

Dixie stopped dead in her tracks. Tears rolled down her cheeks. She hugged herself, trying to stop the convulsions she'd held at bay for the last thirty minutes. She couldn't remember a time in her life when she'd been that scared. She covered her mouth as a guttural sob erupted in her throat.

The ambulance blipped the siren before taking off down the street, the cop car following behind.

Deep down, she knew this wasn't her fault. However, she couldn't help but feel responsible. Whatever happened to Elle, happened on Dixie's watch and by the disappointed glare Kent had given her, he held her accountable. She glanced over her shoulder. She probably would have felt the same way if the tables were turned and it was her Nicky who had been in that ambulance.

She made her way back inside and started cleaning. That poor girl. There was vomit everywhere, and Dixie wasn't sure she'd ever be able to get the smell out.

"Mommy," Nicky stood in front her, rubbing his sleepy eyes. "Where's Elle? She's not in her bed."

Dixie gathered up all the dirty towels and the clothes she'd been wearing when Elle had gotten sick, stuffing them in a laundry basket. She took Nicky by the hand and led him through the family room. Never in a million years would she ever think she'd want a washer and dryer in the kitchen, but hell, this worked. She took her phone out of her back pocket. Still no message from Kent on Elle's condition. She kept telling herself no news was good news. Besides, it had only been about thirty minutes since the ambulance took her away.

"Climb up on the chair while I get you some cereal."

He sucked on his quivering lower lip. "Did they both leave?"

"No, baby, not like you think." She sat down next to Nicky, rubbing his back. "Elle got sick. Really sick and she had to go to the hospital."

"Is Kent with her?"

Dixie nodded as she swallowed the lump in her throat. "Why don't you draw Elle a picture, and we can drive over to the hospital later and see how she's doing."

Nicky nodded.

She poured him a bowl of cereal and set down some markers and a piece of paper. As soon as she finished the laundry, she'd head over to the hospital, even if she hadn't heard anything from Kent.

outine surgery.

There was nothing routine about having to slice open a child and remove their appendix.

Kent paced in the waiting room. It had been sixty-seven minutes since they took her into the operating room. They told him the surgery wouldn't take longer than an hour as long as there were no complications.

The doors swished open and Kent snapped his head toward the sound, but it wasn't the doctor and it wasn't Dixie.

Where the fuck was she? Instinctively, he reached in his back pocket, but he'd left his phone in the station house. Didn't matter. If she cared, she would have been minutes behind him. He took in a deep calming breath. She did have Nicky to deal with, but really, it had been two hours since he and Elle had arrived at the hospital.

"Mr. Carter?" A man in scrubs entered the waiting area. "I'm Josh. I was the nurse in with Elle during her surgery."

"She's out? How is she?" His pulse beat so fast he thought for sure he'd drop dead of a heart attack right there. He blinked, trying to clear the sudden double vision.

"She's fine." Josh rested a firm hand on Kent's shoulder. "No complications and we're expecting to be able to send her home tomorrow."

That seemed soon, but then again, Kent had already gotten cleared for a week off, so he'd have no problem taking care of his little girl. "Can I see her?"

"You sure can. She's still groggy and might fall asleep a lot over the next few hours."

Kent willed his heart rate to settle down. He didn't want Elle to see how shaken up he'd been. The stronger he appeared, the faster she'd heal. Well, that's what he told himself.

"She did make one request of you, though."

"What's that?"

"She asked me to tell you not to call her Buttercup."

Kent shook his head. "I've been calling her that since the day she was born. Kind of a hard habit to break."

"Take it from a father of three teenage daughters. Unless you're handing them the keys to your car or a credit card, it's best to stick with their given name."

Opening and closing his hands, Kent slowly rid himself of the tension that had all his muscles tied up in knots. "Do they ever stop rolling their eyes?"

"My oldest is seventeen and she's the worst, but my favorite is the foot stomp while yelling, 'Daddy, you never let me do anything. You're the meanest.' All followed by a hair flip, long sigh, and a slammed door. Ten minutes later, she's all, 'Daddy, I love you, can I have twenty dollars?'" Josh shook his head, laughing. "It never gets easier; it just gets different."

"Not sure that makes me feel any better."

Josh slapped him on the back as they turned the corner. "I've got all girls, and I can't imagine life any differently. Oh, before I forget, Elle keeps asking for Dixie. Is she somewhere in the hospital where I can track her down?"

"She's at home. I'm hoping she'll be here

soon, though." The fog started to lift from Kent's brain as he recalled the events since he'd heard the call over the station radio, before he saw Dixie's text. Everything between the time he heard his address and this moment had been one big blur. "Is there a phone I can use? I left mine at the station." Only, he didn't remember Dixie's number.

"You can use the one at the nurses' station." Josh stopped at a door. A whiteboard with Elle Carter written in black ink hung from a hook. "I'm on duty till five tonight, so if you need anything at all, just let me or one of the other nurses know."

"Thanks." On his tiptoes, Kent made his way to his daughter's bedside. Tears burned his eyes as he watched a machine pulse with her heartbeat. An IV hung from a metal rack above her head, the tubing circling down to where a needle had been threaded into a vein on the top of her hand.

Her head flopped in his direction, and a bright smile spread across her cheeks. "Hi, Daddy," she said with a hoarse voice.

Leaning over, he kissed her temple, fanning his hand over the top of her head. "My darling Elle," he whispered. "You gave me quite the scare." He sat on the edge of the bed, holding her hand.

"I didn't mean to." Her eyelids fluttered heavily over her almond eyes.

"Well, we can't control a burst appendix."

"It was horrible, and I got sick all over Dixie."

Lifting his hand, he squeezed the bridge of his nose. That had to be the worst smell on the planet. "It's over now, and in a few weeks, you'll be running around like nothing happened."

A couple of taps echoed off the wood door. Josh peeked his head in. "Sorry to bother you, but Dixie is here."

Finally.

"Unfortunately, we can't let small children in," Josh said.

"Daddy, I want to see Dixie," Elle's voice quivered as if it were laced with tears.

"I'll go watch Nicky so she can visit." He kissed her, giving her hand a good squeeze. Exhaustion from being up for over twenty-four hours kicked in. His eyes burned, and he suspected they were blood-shot as all hell.

Nurses and doctors hustled about the corridor. The smell of antiseptic made his stomach clench as it begged for food.

"Kent!" Nicky jumped up and down and around in a circle before bolting down the hallway.

"Stop," Dixie called, but Nicky obviously wasn't going to take heed as he flung himself into Kent's outstretched arms.

"Hey there, little man, how are you?"

Nothing like having plump little fingers wrapped around your neck as a toddler attempted a big bear hug. Kent closed his eyes, taking in the fresh scent of baby soap.

"How is she?" the voice of an angel asked.

He blinked open his eyes and once again, Dixie sucked out all the oxygen from his lungs. Her long blond hair cascaded over her shoulders. Her indigo eyes twinkled under the florescent lighting.

"She's really good," he said, shifting Nicky to his hip. "She'd like to see you."

"You don't mind watching Nicky for a couple of minutes?"

He narrowed his eyes. "Of course not."

"I won't be long." She shot past him like a lightning bolt, scurrying down the hallway, clutching her purse in one hand, a piece of paper flying in the other.

"Can we go play with the blocks?" Nicky kicked his feet.

"Where did you see toys?"

Nicky pointed to a room not far from the nurses' station.

"Sounds good to me." Kent glanced over his shoulder once, but Dixie had already disappeared down the hall. He ran his palm down the side of his cheek, the stubble scratching his calloused skin.

He got down on the ground, sitting cross-legged as he helped Nicky stack the blocks on top of each other. "So, what have you and your mom been doing this morning?" God, he was pathetic. Resorting to grilling a toddler to find out where Dixie had been.

"Mommy did laundry because Elle got sick on everything." Nicky glanced up with a scrunched face as if he'd eaten something sour. "And it smelled worse than poop."

Kent chuckled. "I bet. Did you do anything else?"

"I made a picture for Elle of her and me playing in the sandbox."

"She'll love that." Kent held a block between his fingers. He studied the rounded edges, contemplating his next question. It's not like Dixie could have done anything, except maybe sit with him, but he supposed having a toddler hanging around a hospital probably wasn't the best plan.

"Did Mommy say anything about me?" Did he really just ask a three-year-old that question?

Nicky lifted a block and pretended to fly it through the air, making engine noises. "She said a bad word."

"Sometimes mommies do that." Kent tried to pull his pride out of his ass, but he'd gone so far down the rabbit hole, there was no coming back. They'd barely shared two kisses and attraction doesn't make for good companionship, a lesson he'd learned the hard way. He had a kid and a career, and she had a life to get back on track. Neither one of them had any time to even explore any kind of feelings they might have for one another. He patted Nicky on the head, giving his hair a good ruffle. The longer he stuck around, the more he'd end up hurting this little boy, and he wouldn't be able to live with himself.

He was going to have to ease himself out of Nicky's life. Maybe not completely, since he'd told Jackie it was fine with him if she babysat him and his daughter, but still, there was no point in entertaining this train of thought anymore.

The smell of sweet citrus filled his nostrils right before Dixie strolled into the family waiting area.

"Thanks for watching him." She stood with her hands on her hips.

"Not a problem." Kent jumped to his feet. "Can I talk to you for a minute?"

She glanced at her watch. "I've got to get going. My aunt called, and she's coming home tomorrow, so I need to run a few errands and clean up the house."

He tilted his head. "Why are you mad? If anyone should be mad, it's me."

"You're kidding, right?" She narrowed her eyes.

"No. I'm not. It's been a long morning, and I can't imagine what I've done to deserve the cold shoulder."

She narrowed her eyes into tiny slits. Her lips pulled tight. "You really don't know?"

"Enlighten me."

"I don't have the time for this," she said, her gaze shifting to Nicky. "Put the blocks down, buddy. It's time to go."

"Wait a second." He coiled his fingers around her biceps.

She jerked her arm away.

Holding his hands to his sides, he said, "I just want to hold true to the promise I made to Nicky about fishing. I don't want to be just another asshole who disappoints him."

She huffed out a breath. "I appreciate that. Just let me know when it works for you, and if it's okay with you, I'd like to come visit Elle tomorrow after Jackie lands."

"They might send her home tomorrow but come whenever you like. Bring Nicky whether it be here or my place. I'll take him for a ride on the Harley."

She nodded. "Just answer my texts this time." She bent over and picked up a protesting Nicky.

"What does that mean?"

"It would have been nice to know what was wrong with Elle. I had no idea until I got here and I wasn't even sure I was wanted. But I was sick with worry. I'd never seen so much vomit come from one little girl."

"Oh. I'm sorry. I left my phone at the station, or I would have."

She pursed her lips, shaking her head. "There are a million phones around here you could have used. Nicky, say goodbye to Kent."

Nicky leaned over his mother's shoulder as she walked away, waving frantically.

"I don't have your phone number memorized."

"I've got yours memorized." She flipped her hand in the air. "But you had that as a priority on your lists, which I did read, by the way."

"I'm sorry. I'll work on it," he called to the back of her hair. "We're good? You're not mad anymore?" God, he wished she would just turn around.

"That was only half the reason."

"What's the other half?"

He scratched the back of his head as she entered the elevator, mentally going over everything he could recall from the day's events. It had all a haze. He remembered seeing the ambulance, which squeezed the air right out of his lungs. When he saw his daughter sprawled out on a gurney, his knees went weak. All he wanted to do was be by her side, and he'd barreled through anything to get to her…

Well, fuck.

What an asshole he'd been. Of course she was mad. He'd not only shoved her out of the way, but he never once said thank you for taking such good care of his Buttercup.

Flowers. He'd send her flowers.

And chocolate. That should be a good start at making things up to her.

At least he knew Jackie's address.

Didn't he?

8

Dixie curled up on the sofa with a box of her favorite chocolates, thanks to Kent, and her favorite housewife show. She'd forgive him for the lack of communication. If the tables were turned, calling him might have been the last thing she thought of, especially if she didn't have her phone. She even had to admit, if only to herself, that she could have easily elbowed anyone, including him, if they stood between her and her sick child.

Ding-dong.

She jumped. The digital clock blinked nine thirty. Who the hell would just stop by at this time of night?

Leaning over the sofa, she glanced out the

window, relieved and annoyed to see Kent's car parked on the street. Her heart fluttered as if she were about to go on her very first car date. Her palms lined with clammy perspiration. But her mind tried to hold on to being angry just a little while longer.

Just to be safe, she peered through the peephole and sighed. On the other side of the door, Kent stood with a dozen carnations in one hand and a little fire truck in the other.

"Why aren't you with Elle at the hospital?" she asked, taking the flowers he offered and bringing them to her nose. She couldn't remember a time, other than her father, where a man had sent her flowers. The gesture was something she could get used to.

"They kicked me out. Something about me needing rest and Elle needing rest, and I wasn't doing her any good being exhausted, hovering over her."

She patted his arm, admiring his thick biceps. "They're right, but how did Elle feel about that?"

"She rolled her eyes and agreed with them."

"She'll be fine. Why don't you sit down while I put these in some water and get you a drink?"

"Before you do that, I need to say something."

He cupped her chin, leaning so close his hot breath tickled her cheek. "I'm sorry. I was just so scared. I had no idea what had happened other than an ambulance had been dispatched to my house."

"It's okay. I get it."

"Do you want to know something crazy?"

"Sure." She tried to tear her gaze from his dark eyes stained with the color of cocoa on a cold winter's night, wrapping you with the warmth of a fleece blanket in front of a roaring fire, making you feel as though you were right where you belonged.

"I wondered why you hadn't shown up at the hospital. When I was alone with Nicky, I kept asking him questions about what you'd done all morning."

She cocked her head, deciding if she should get mad all over again or if what he'd done had been sweet. "And what did he tell you?"

"Just that you're the kindest, most generous woman that ever lived."

"He said no such thing," she said, letting out a slight laugh, until she realized that Kent meant the words. She cleared her throat.

He scowled. "Maybe not in so many words, but it's true." He fanned his thumb over her cheek. "Thank you for being there for Elle."

They stood there for a long, awkward moment as if they were playing the staring game with flowers and a toy truck between them. His tongue parted his lips as he slowly licked them.

"Sit. I'll be right back," she said, needing a little space to calm her raging hormones. He didn't need a chick throwing herself at him. He needed a friend to lean on, and she could do that. Actually, that was all she was going to allow. Didn't matter that he made her all tingly inside or that when she closed her eyes, she could see herself in his arms as she gently drifted off to sleep.

Stop that thinking.

She snagged a vase, filling it with water. After arranging the flowers, she turned and set them on the table. Out of the corner of her eye, movement caught her attention.

"Oh," she whispered, staring at Kent as he sauntered around the table. "Have you slept at all? You really need to get some rest." Her words staggered out of her mouth like a drunken sailor.

"I'll sleep later," he murmured, circling his arms around her waist. "Where's Nicky?"

"Asleep in his room, why?" She leaned back, but that only forced her to grip his shoulders as his lips came closer and closer.

"Tell me to stop. Tell me that this is crazy. That we should stay away from each other."

"Okay," she whispered, breathing in his musky, pine scent that made her muscles turn to jelly. A faint moan glided across her lips.

"I need you to tell me." His lips were scant centimeters from hers. His hot breath excited her skin, sending messages to every erogenous zone she had.

She shuddered, digging her fingernails into his skin. He held her gaze, patiently waiting for her to say something, but her mouth couldn't form any words. Lots of people with children developed long-lasting, loving relationships. It wasn't like she didn't understand Elle came first in his life, and Nicky in hers. They were two adults, needing adult companionship.

"I don't want to tell you to stop," she whispered, trying to take a deep breath, but her lungs were unable to fully expand. "I want you."

He groaned as his lips crash-landed on hers, his tongue darting in her mouth, finding every hot nook and cranny. His hands roamed her ass, squeezing gently before gliding down the back of her thighs. He hoisted her legs around his waist. "Where's your bedroom?"

"Behind us. Second door on the right."

"Does it have a lock?"

She pulled back. "It does, but I've never locked it in case Nicky needs me."

"I won't stay all night." He pushed open the door, gently setting her down on the small bed. "So, it will only be locked while absolutely necessary."

As he attended to the lock on the door, she shook out her hands, waggling her fingers. Goose-bumps lined her flesh. At twenty-three, she had very little experience sexually and as she watched the way he removed his shirt, she suspected he might be a master in bed. She swallowed.

"I just thought of something," he said, his tall, broad body leaning against the door.

"What?" her voice squeaked.

"I don't have any condoms." He tossed his shirt on the desk in the corner and planted his hands on his hips just over where his jeans hugged his body.

Her stomach lurched forward like the finest BMW going from zero to sixty in five seconds flat. "I do."

He arched his right brow, and the corner of his mouth followed in a sexy curve. "You don't say."

Embarrassment flushed her cheeks. "I bought

them after I had Nicky as kind of a reminder of what happens when you have unprotected sex."

"With a son like that, I'd want to toss the birth control out the window and have a dozen more."

The moon shined through the window, casting a warm glow across his tanned skin. She reached out, touching the spot between his pecs where a trickle of hair gathered, fingering the curls.

"He is pretty perfect." Kneeling on the bed, she kissed the side of his neck. "And you're sweet to say something so nice, but—"

"Don't worry. Condom it is. I'm just saying that you're the kind of woman who could steal my heart." He traced his thumb over her lower lip. "Then again, I might just hand it to you on a silver platter."

"Do you always butter up the ladies when they're already willing?" Before she lost her nerve, she slipped her shirt over her head. Her nipples tightened in the air-conditioning.

A deep growl echoed in her ears. "Do you always go braless?"

"Only when I go to bed." With a shot of bravery, she took his hand and rested his palm over her breasts.

"Dear God, woman, you're going to kill me."

His thumb dragged over the tight nub, rolling gently.

She arched her back, biting down on her lower lip. A million firecrackers imploded over her skin with the promise of grand fireworks to light up her insides like the night sky on the Fourth of July. With every moist touch of his lips and tongue, her need grew. Desperation raced through her veins, pumping through her heart, demanding she take her fill for the very first time. She clawed and groped at his bare chest.

"Whoa," she said with a heavy breath as he tossed her on her back and yanked her sweats to her ankles.

"Jesus, no panties either?"

"Not when I go… Oh my God," she bit down on her hand as his tongue dived deep between her legs.

He knelt on the floor beside the bed, hoisting her legs over his shoulders, his hand gripping her ass, kneading her skin while his mouth did things to her she'd never imagined. It wasn't that she'd never had oral sex before—of course she had—but the few men she'd been with didn't worship her like a goddess. Kent moved over her with the same exultant desire she craved. Every stroke… every lick… every touch served to excite and satisfy.

Fisting the sheets, she dug her heels into his shoulders, pushing away only to bring him back in with a roll of her hips. His hot breath coated her like fudge dripping over ice cream.

His eyelids fluttered open, his bourbon eyes filling her, making her drunk on his love. He reached up, covering her mouth with one hand while the other slipped inside, rubbing swiftly as he sucked hard on her swollen nub.

She pounded the mattress, thrusting her hips upward, groaning into his hand, fighting the urge to bite the soft swell of his palm.

The room spun, and she felt dizzy, like she'd been on the highest, fastest roller coaster of all time, kicking her adrenaline into high gear, allowing exhilaration to take over her mind, body, and soul. Just when she thought it couldn't get any better, he shifted slightly, changing the angle of his fingers and the pressure of his mouth, sending her into outer space at Mach five.

"Oh… oh…" She clutched his head with both hands; her stomach seized with tremors, jerking her forward. Warmth poured out of her body like a waterfall at a hot spring. She could feel the heat rise like steam, drenching them with pleasure.

She stared down at him kissing her inner thigh while she urgently tried to catch her breath. Her lungs burned as if she'd landed on her back, knocking the wind out of her.

His hand flattened over her stomach. "Are you okay?" He kissed the space between her breasts.

She nodded like an idiot, heaving in breaths as if she were hyperventilating.

"I think someone liked that," he mused with a wicked smile.

"Ya think," she managed between pants.

"We can end there, if you want."

"Hell no," she said a little too quickly.

He chuckled. "I'm terrified I just set the standard too high, and I'll never be able to make your body do that again."

"We won't know unless we try." She slipped her hand into the front of his pants, grazing him with her thumb. "We need you out of these constricting clothes."

"I'm not going to argue." He stood and quickly dropped his pants to the floor, exposing his body in all its splendor.

"Jesus, you're beautiful," she mumbled, taking

him into her hands. Sex had never been an empowering act before. It had been something she did, trying to seek pleasure. Her body knew it was there, she'd felt it when alone in the bath, but no man had ever given her the kind of gratification that made her want to do whatever it took to make sure they shuddered with the same bliss. She wanted to make him dizzy with desire. Drunk with need.

She took as much of him as she could in her mouth, her hands following, stroking tightly, then soft like a feather. Exploring every inch, she thought only about indulging his cravings. Forgetting about her inhibitions, she cupped him and clasped her mouth around him, letting her teeth graze against his soft, sensitive skin.

His groans and hisses filled the air, and she wanted more. She wanted to play his body like a fine instrument.

"Dixie," he said with a deep groan. "Where are the condoms?"

She slipped her mouth off him, still holding him tightly in her hands, licking her lips, smiling, feeling like the sexiest, most desirable woman that ever breathed.

"You are going to kill me." He reached down,

tilting her chin with his thumb. "Where are they before I explode right here?"

"Nightstand."

He batted her hands away, gently pushing her back on the mattress.

Watching his muscles flex as he reached across the bed made her skin prickle with heat. She propped herself on her elbows, heels into the bed, legs slightly spread. Her wariness disappeared as she sheathed him with protection.

He growled as he nestled himself between her legs, biting at her lower lip. "You have no idea how mad with lust you make me."

"Why don't you show me?" She raised her hips slightly, letting the length of him caress her. "Oh, Kent," she said with a moan as he slid himself inside her in one long, slow stroke. She raised her legs, clasping her ankles at the small of his back. Her hips rocked back and forth, meeting his every plunge deep inside her.

He rose up, his hands pressed on the bed on either side of her head. He stared at her with his pools of dark-cinnamon swirls that carried the depth and desire that could only come from having loved so deeply that it took a piece of your soul.

She swallowed as he tenderly kissed her nose and cheek.

The rhythm of his lovemaking didn't slow, but it did change. It shifted from raw energy to something akin to utter devotion. She clamped around him, letting her climax propel to the surface. She shuddered, drawing him in deeper, needing to feel him swell inside her and release his pleasure. She urgently needed to know she had the ability to give him the most decadent experience he could possibly have.

He thrust harder and faster. "Dixie," he whispered, still holding her gaze. "Beautiful Dixie." Burying his face in her neck, he sucked on her earlobe, pumping frantically.

"Yes," she said, holding him tight.

He let out a guttural groan as he twitched inside her, sending a mini shock wave through her system. For the next few minutes, they rocked slowly against one another, her hand roaming his back, his lips kissing her neck.

She accepted his full weight, relaxing into the bed.

"You're way out of my league," he whispered.

"You're way too sweet."

"I have my moments." He rolled to his side,

pulling the blanket over their sweat-covered bodies. Propped up on his elbow, he stared at her, tracing her lips with his index finger. "I've never met anyone like you before."

"I hope that's a good thing."

He laughed. "It's a great thing." He batted her nose. "I need to check my phone, just to make sure the hospital isn't trying to reach me."

While she completely understood, the gravity of the situation hit her full force. Others might be able to blend families, and it might work out just fine, but she wasn't sure she could do it, and she knew Kent couldn't. He was good with Nicky, but Elle was his flesh and blood.

"Go right ahead," she said, expecting him to get out of bed and get dressed. But all he did was lean over the side and rummage through his jeans.

"No messages. That has to be a good thing."

"Does she have her phone?"

He nodded, slipping his arm around her, pulling her head to his chest. "I feel like if I leave you right now I'm being a bigger asshole than I was earlier."

She kissed his pec, forcing any negative thought she had to the recesses of her mind. "I need you to leave. It's not about you, but about my son."

"Believe me, I understand. If we were at my

house, I'd be asking you to leave for the very same reasons. But it doesn't make me feel any better about it."

She took in a deep breath, letting it out slowly. "It's probably best if we say good night now before we both fall asleep."

"All right."

They got dressed in silence, though he tried to convince her to stay in bed, but she needed to lock up behind him.

Leaning against the front door, she watched his hips sway in a masculine swagger, his jeans riding low and loose. He turned once and waved, before sliding into the front seat of his car. She stood there for a good five minutes after he drove off before shutting off the lights and heading back to bed.

Her phone beeped on the nightstand.

Kent: *Good night, Dixie. Sleep well and dream of me.*

She couldn't let that go unanswered.

Dixie: *Right back at you. Call me in the morning and let me know when and where I can come visit with Elle.*

Kent: *Will do. XOXO*

Dixie: *XOXO*

She set her phone on the table and curled up on her bed, hugging her pillow, inhaling the fresh scent of pine. He always smelled like a forest and she wanted to run wild in one with him at her side. She let out a big sigh. She was in way over her head, and she was going to get hurt. She could handle that, as long as Elle and Nicky were protected. She'd do anything for those children.

The next two weeks went by in a blur. Kent spent most of his time tending to his daughter. Actually, it was more like trying to tie her down so she got the proper rest she needed. The doctor said she'd heal quickly, and at the last visit, he told them she could continue to increase her activity, depending on her pain level.

And then there was Dixie, who had started her new job. They had been able to occasionally sneak some alone time. A stolen moment for a bike ride at sunset or a quick kiss while no one was looking, but they hadn't been able to be intimate with each other again, and it was driving Kent absolutely mad. He craved to hold her in his arms until she fell asleep. To watch the sun peek through the window, kissing her blond hair and watching her eyes flutter open so he was the first thing she'd see in the morning.

She'd been the only woman he'd ever met whom he couldn't stop thinking about. She'd seep into his thoughts at random moments, making him smile. His crew chief, Arthur, twice the other day tossed a paperclip at him during a meeting, telling him to wipe the stupid grin off his face.

"Daddy, you're burning the French toast," Elle said, poking his biceps.

"Sorry." Quickly, he flipped the fluffy, but slightly crispy bread on the griddle. He'd been dealing with a lack of sexual activity since Elle had been born, but now that he'd had the kind of mind-numbing sex others bragged about, he couldn't look at Dixie and not want to rip her clothes off and do unspeakable things to her body. No amount of cold showers would cure him of his ailment. Only Dixie could take care of that.

And that was another issue. There would never be another woman for him, ever. She was it. The cream of the crop. His soulmate.

"Dad!" Elle grabbed the spatula from his hand. "What is the matter with you?" she asked in a tone indicative of a mother scolding a small child.

"Sorry, my mind is in other places."

"Obviously," she said, shoving him aside. "You can set the table, and I'll finish up here. When is Dixie and Nicky coming over?"

"They said nine thirty, so about twenty minutes," he said. He'd been looking forward to fishing with Nicky for weeks, and he knew his daughter was over the moon about a mani-pedi, whatever that meant, followed by a hair appointment.

But when the day was done, Jackie had promised to take the kids for the night, giving him and Dixie a chance to spend some quality alone time together. Dixie had balked at the idea, but he suspected she was more concerned about what her aunt thought of her spending the night with him. Jackie appeared to be more than thrilled with the concept, telling him she herself couldn't have picked a better boyfriend for her niece. However, the jury was still out on his relationship status.

And with good reason.

They needed to take a step back and then move slowly going forward, making sure their children were protected. It wasn't that they didn't want to be together, but they had things in their lives that came first.

And then there was the question about Nicky's father, who could come waltzing into their lives at any moment wreaking havoc, turning their worlds upside down. That thought reminded him of the recent email he'd sent Darius.

Sitting at the table, he pulled out his cell phone. His heart hammered with twinges of guilt. He knew, without a doubt, Dixie would not appreciate him poking around in her background, much less Daniel's.

His phone icon indicated someone had left him a text message. He tapped on it and then on Darius' number.

Hey, Kent. I've got some good news, bad news, and worse news. The good news is I found Daniel. The bad news is he's running drugs for Pepe Fernandez out of Miami. The worse news is he was in Rivera Beach last night, and I got word he's headed north this morning on 95. The Feds have been trying to bring down Pepe for months now. His pipeline runs from Miami to Fort Bragg. Daniel is a new runner for them, so I tipped off the Feds, but I'd watch your back.

Fucking wonderful. The only way Daniel was ever getting to Nicky again was through Kent, and that wasn't ever going to happen.

"Don't roll your eyes, Daddy."

To try and lighten his now soured mood, he rolled them again.

"If you can do it, then so can I."

He waggled his finger toward his daughter. "This is not a case of monkey see, monkey do."

"Of course not. It's a double standard for grown-ups just like it is between men and women."

He opened and closed his mouth a few times before his brain could process the adult conversation he was having with a ten-year-old. "What double standards between boys and girls?"

She set the two nearly burnt pieces on his plate with some sausages and settled into the chair next to him with the perfectly good pieces. Well, she had cooked them, and he'd cooked the not-so-great ones.

"If girls are assertive and speak their minds, they are seen as bossy, or that *B* word. But if men are that way, they are considered the future leaders. Women aren't given the same opportunities as men just because we're girls."

He waved his fork. "The world is changing, and you're making a blanket statement. Women can do and be anything."

"Oh, come on, Daddy. How many female

generals are there? How many women do you work with at the fire station or at the Aegis Network?" She smiled triumphantly, popping a sausage link in her mouth.

"There are some women and it's constantly changing."

She raised her hand in the air. "But there's still a double standard. We live in such a patri… patri-art…" She looked up at the ceiling as if the word would drop down from the sky.

"Patriarchal?" he asked.

"That's what I was trying to say. Our society is based on the idea that women are less than men."

"That was a long time ago and not true. Women are equal to men, just our bodies are different."

She lowered her chin and glared at him. "Let me finish, Dad."

He nodded, still trying to figure out when his daughter had turned into a debate queen.

"No matter how far we've come, it's still a patriarchal society, and men are just given more opportunities than women."

"You're right," he admitted, though this wasn't a conversation he ever imagined having with his kid, but he certainly enjoyed it. "Where are you learning all this?"

"A book I'm reading that I checked out of the digital library. It's all about feminism and the struggles women face in today's world."

He opened his mouth, but she held her hand out.

"It's intended for girls my age, so don't worry."

"Ha!" He reached over, stealing a hunk of her breakfast. "That's not what I was going to say."

"Oh, right." She rolled her eyes.

"Really, sweetheart, this is a good topic to be passionate about. Look at your aunt Tilly and all the good she does with her programs and helping women. We need more people in this world like her."

Elle nodded, chewing her food vigorously. "Dixie loves her new job. When I grow up, I want to do what they are doing."

"Sounds like a good plan, but until then, mind going to back to being Daddy's little girl?"

"I'm going to grow up."

Ding-dong.

"Hello, you guys in here?" Dixie called out.

"In the kitchen."

Nicky's feet hitting the floorboards as he raced through the house sounded like sweet music.

Kent pushed his chair back, waiting for the little boy to see him and jump on his lap. "Hey, little man."

He stopped, raising his arms, making fists and flexing his nonexistent muscles. "I'm a big man," he said in a deep voice.

"That you are." He helped the boy up, who glanced between him and the plate of food. "Have at it, kid." He pulled back the chair next to him for Dixie.

She shook her head. "I need to speak with you for a minute. Alone."

"All right. Elle, watch Nicky, okay?"

Elle nodded as he set Nicky in the booster seat he'd picked up. Poor kid didn't need to eat on his knees every time he came over, even if he didn't seem to mind.

"What's wrong?" Resting his hand on the small of her back, he guided her into the family room, his concern growing as her gaze darted from the door back to his face.

"There was a car outside Jackie's house this morning."

He balled his fists. "Whose car? What kind of car?"

"It's your basic small SUV, dark blue, older model, but well taken care of with tinted windows. I didn't think anything of it at first until it pulled out behind me. Now it's parked down at the corner."

"Stay here and keep the kids inside," he said with a stern tone, one that he normally reserved when training new firefighters.

"What are you going to do?"

"Have a little chat with whoever is in the car."

She grabbed his biceps, squeezing hard. "What if it's—" She gasped, covering her mouth. "It's Daniel," she whispered, pointing to the picture window behind the dark-brown sofa.

He closed his eyes for a brief moment. "Stay in the house," he said behind gritted teeth. "I'll take care of him." Reaching out, he fanned his thumb over her cheekbone and cupped her face. "Don't worry. I'm not going to let him near you or Nicky."

"Is that the right thing to do? He's never laid a hand on me or him. He's not violent."

"Maybe not, but he's doing just as much damage to that little boy as if he were. It would be one thing if he was late on child support but tried to maintain a relationship. However, he hasn't even tried to contact you or his kid. He's no good."

"You're right. You're right." She nodded. "I should have listened to my aunt when Nicky was born. But I wanted so desperately for my son to have two parents."

"Trust me, I can understand that thought. Now let me handle this." He opened and closed his fists, pumped out his chest, and stepped through the front door. "May I help you?"

Daniel stood at the edge of the driveway. His long hair was pulled back into a ponytail. He wore faded jeans, a black T-shirt, and his face was clean-shaven. He looked to be about six foot and muscular.

"Yeah. I want to talk to Dixie."

"She doesn't want to talk to you."

"I want to see my boy," Daniel said, folding his arms and spreading his stance.

"You can take that up with the court system. Oh, wait. You won't do that because you'll get arrested for being a deadbeat dad. Now get the fuck off my property."

Daniel laughed. "Tsk. Tsk. You didn't do your homework. I don't owe any child support because she dropped the ball on that one, setting me free and clear."

"Perhaps, but you have no visitation rights, and you're a drifter with barely two pennies to rub together." Kent took three steps forward, keeping his eyes locked on Daniel.

"You think you know shit about me because you've been poking around my business?"

Kent's breath hitched. Darius was the best at finding people and covering his tracks. He'd found Daniel. Now, how did that little weasel know anyone was snooping into his background? "I'm not sure I understand."

"You've messed with the wrong man. My boss doesn't like it when his employees have people asking around about them."

Shit. Pepe Hernandez was not the kind of man you fucked with.

"Stay away from Dixie and her son, and no one will ever be asking about you again."

Daniel shook his head. "Call off your goons, and I will."

"Done," Kent said, holding his phone. "Just need to make one call."

"Do it, and I'll be gone. If not, I'll be back, and I'll be coming for my boy." With that, Daniel turned on his heel and strolled down the street toward his car without a care in the world.

Anyone who thought they were untouchable was sorely mistaken, and Daniel would rue the day he came anywhere near the people Kent loved.

His heart pounded at the last thought, but he pushed it out of his mind as he took out his phone and texted Darius the license plate number along with a buddy of his from the local police department. Hopefully, they'd be able to get a handle on what this asshole was up to. Until then, he wasn't sure it was safe to go anywhere.

Raking his fingers through his hair, he headed back inside.

"Did you spy on me?" Dixie asked with a hushed tone but an angry one nonetheless.

"I wouldn't call it spying. I did a background check. Any parent would—"

She poked him in the chest. "When someone does a background check on a potential employee, that person generally knows it's happening, and it doesn't include nosing around their loser ex-boyfriend whom they'd prefer not to ever see again."

"Look. Maybe I should have told you I'd be doing that, but—"

"No buts. Your prying brought him here, and you've put me in a horrible situation with my son," she said, still in a menacing whisper. "I'll forgive you for doing a check on me, because I'd do the same thing if I had the resources, but you took it a step too far and you brought Daniel right to my doorstep."

"Kent!" Nicky came barreling into the room, arms flapping.

Kent picked up the little boy and kissed him on the cheek. He'd never let any harm come to him. Ever. That was a promise he intended to keep if it was the last thing he ever did.

"I'm ready to go," Elle said, looping her arm through Dixie's, who stared at him with a sadness that stabbed him right through his heart.

"There has been a change in plans," he said quietly, holding Dixie's gaze.

"What!" Elle's smile quickly turned to a pout.

"A situation has come up that I can't discuss in certain company." He nodded his head toward Nicky who'd become amused by the tattoo on Kent's neck. "Until I hear back from a friend, we're going to have to stay put."

Elle stomped her foot. "You've got to be kidding me. You promised, Dad, and you rarely break your word unless it's work-related or someone died. Is it one of those two things?"

"No." He held up a hand. "I intend to keep that promise, just not this minute," Kent said.

"When then, Dad?" Elle pushed out her hip. "It's not just me you're letting down." She wiggled her finger at Nicky. "He wanted to go…" She mouthed the word *fishing*.

"I understand, and hopefully, in an hour or two. I need you to be patient. Can you do that for me?"

"Why don't we go to your room, and I'll curl your hair like the girl on the show you like so much while we wait for your father to find out what he needs. And if not today, we will have our girls' day another time." Dixie smoothed down Elle's hair with the tender care only a mother could. "I'm pretty good with makeup too."

"None of that," Kent said. "She's too young."

"Not today, she's not." Dixie glared. "And I'm not arguing with you about it."

"Okay," Elle said less than enthusiastically, tugging Dixie across the room.

"Looks like it's just you and me, pal, for the next hour or so. What shall we do?"

Nicky shrugged. "I don't know."

"I've got it." Kent set Nicky down, holding his

hand. "Let's clean out the fishing box so that when it's time to go, we'll be all ready." He glanced at his phone. All he needed to know was that Daniel was miles away, hopefully never to return.

He brought the fishing kit out to the garage, setting it up on the ground. He'd bought a few new lures, different-size weights, and a couple of bobbers. "All right, Nicky, you take these round weights and put the tiny ones in this spot, the middle-sized ones here, and these big ones in this spot. Got it?"

Nicky nodded, his pudgy fingers plucking the silver beads from the floor and plopping them in their spots, just like Kent had instructed.

Anger and frustration swirled in Kent's gut. He'd never understand men like Daniel. It was one thing not to be in love with Nicky's mother. Kent hadn't loved Elle's. He tried like hell to after he'd found out she was pregnant, but it just wasn't there.

But no way could he ever not want Elle in his life.

A door slammed, followed by a crash sound from inside the house. Quickly, he scooped up Nicky. "Elle? Dixie? Everything okay in here?" He sucked in a harsh breath, staring at two men with guns, holding the wide-eyed girls, tears streaking their cheeks. He shielded Nicky's face. "Who are you, and what do you want?"

"Who we are is immaterial," the man holding his daughter said. He wore a blue T-shirt and had a scar on his face.

Kent made mental notes of the tattoos he could see, trying to engrave the man's face in his brain.

"But we want Daniel and the money he stole from our boss," the man with the scar said.

"He left about an hour ago. No idea where he went." Kent wanted to add that he couldn't care less about Daniel but didn't know if Nicky knew his father's first name or not.

Nicky squirmed, trying to turn his body. "Is that a real gun?" he asked.

"I need you to be still and keep your eyes closed, can you do that?" he whispered into the little boy's ear.

Nicky buried his face in Kent's neck, fingering the tattoo.

"Can we let my girlfriend take the kids into the other room, and we can discuss this outside?"

"No can do," the man with the scar said. "When we get our shit back, then we let them go."

"Take me instead." Kent knew these men wouldn't go for that, but he had to try.

"Stop negotiating or we'll take the little boy too. He's more valuable anyway."

Dixie cried out, her shoulders bumping up and down.

The man with the red T-shirt yanked her hair. "Be quiet."

Kent tried to shield Nicky, holding him tight against his chest. "I'm going to pull out my phone and call one of my buddies who's tracking him."

The man with the scar cocked his head. "Why?"

"We want him out of our lives, so I'm making sure that happens." He glanced between his daughter and the woman he knew without a doubt he wanted to spend the rest of his life with. His gaze pleaded with them both to trust him.

Holding Nicky with one hand, he reached into his back pocket and pulled out his phone. "I'll put it on speaker," he said.

"If you signal them about us, she bites the bullet." The man holding Dixie shoved his gun against her temple. "Then we'll hurt the girl."

Kent exhaled through his nose like a bull as he tapped on his phone. Darius picked up on the first ring.

"I was just about to call you," Darius said.

"Just watch what you say, I'm in the car on speaker with little ears."

"Hey, Elle, how are you doing?"

Kent nodded to his daughter.

"I'm good," she said with a shaky voice and a sniffle.

"I don't have much time and wondered if you had any news to report on our friend."

"As a matter of fact, I just heard he got off 95 about twenty minutes from you. He's loading stuff in a four-door sedan. Timothy has eyes on him," Darius said.

"Did he have help?"

"Not that Timothy saw. What's going on?" Darius asked.

"Nothing. Just a few more friends looking for him. Can you send me what you have and our friend's location so I can give it to them?" Kent honestly didn't care he was tossing Daniel under the bus. Only Daniel had better hope that the cops would get him before these thugs did, or he might not see the sun rise tomorrow.

"I'll do it right now."

"Great. I've got to go." Kent tapped the phone at the same time it buzzed. He tossed the cell on the table. "There's all the information for you to find him. Now let my girls go and leave my house."

Nicky's fingers clasped behind Kent's neck, and his body shivered. He had no idea what he understood, but he got the sense more than he should.

"Nope." The man with the scar snagged his phone. "What's the passcode?"

"9845," Kent said.

The two men inched toward the back door, pulling his precious Elle and sweet Dixie with them. "Once we have our man and our product, we'll let them go, unharmed." He raised his brow. "But if we don't, well, you know how that goes."

"We'll be in touch," the other man said.

Kent lunged forward but halted the second a gun pointed in his direction.

"I'm not afraid to shoot you and if I do, the bullet goes through the boy. I don't think you want that."

Kent watched in horror as the two men walked through the side gate and got into a van that had been parked on the side street, stuffing Dixie and Elle into the back seat.

"Echo, Charlie, Delta, seven, seven, Oscar," he mumbled the license plate number. Clinging to a sobbing Nicky, he ran back into the kitchen, looking for either Elle's phone or Dixie's. He found Dixie's on the kitchen counter, locked.

"Damn," he muttered. He rubbed Nicky's back. "Do you know how to get into Mommy's phone?"

"I do." Nicky took her phone in his little hands, and he swiped his fingers across the number pad.

"Thank you."

"That didn't look like a girl's day."

"It's going to be okay, little man."

Time to call in the cavalry.

10

Dixie wrapped her arms around Elle's trembling body in the back of a white van. Guilt plagued her mind. None of this had been Kent's fault, and she'd all but blamed him and now she and his daughter were being held at gunpoint.

"I'm scared," Elle whimpered.

"I know, sweetie." Dixie smoothed down Elle's hair, tucking her head into Dixie's chest as the child sobbed uncontrollably. "Your dad is going to find us."

"What do those men want?"

"I'm not exactly sure, but someone I used to know showed up today, and I think he has something they want."

Elle tipped her head. Her normally happy toffee eyes had turned a cold brown filled with fear. "But what does that have to do with us?"

Dixie had no idea how to answer that question. If she told Elle the truth about Nicky's father, then her son would probably find out, and it was hard enough to find answers about why his father left.

"It has nothing to do with you."

The back doors swung open.

"Let's go," one of her captors said, showing his gun. This man was the meaner of the two. He had piercing blue eyes that were lined with deep-set wrinkles. "Be quiet, and don't say a word."

Elle shook violently.

"I've got you, sweetie." Dixie's heart pounded like a jackhammer, but she needed to be strong for Elle. Holding her tightly, Dixie helped her from the van. She looked around, straining to see the street sign a few houses away. The homes were run-down, and most of the grass and bushes were overgrown. There was a random solar window shop across the street.

Her captor held her by the arm, guiding them toward an old blue home with weeds as tall as Nicky swaying in the breeze. The picture window in the front of the house was covered with a thick layer of dirt. They walked around to the backyard. The door to a back patio rattled, hanging open.

"Get inside."

The floorboards creaked under the weight of her steps. A musty stench filled her nose, causing her to sneeze. The house smelled like death and animal droppings. The other man who had taken them sat at the kitchen table with his nose in a tablet. He'd been kinder, offering them a tissue for Elle, but that didn't make him a good man since he'd shoved a gun in the poor child's face.

"Take a seat over there," the blue-eyed man said, pushing them toward a couch.

Elle cried out, clutching her side.

"I'd appreciate it if you stopped manhandling her." Dixie eased Elle onto the sagging sofa covered by an old crochet afghan.

"Oh, you would now," Blue Eyes said.

Elle coughed.

Dixie cradled Elle's head in her lap, stroking her soft brown hair. "Can we get some water?"

"I wouldn't drink the water in this place," the other man said, lifting his gaze from the screen in his hands. "But you can have this." He picked up a half-empty water bottle and tossed it.

Thankfully, she caught it before it landed on Elle's face.

Dixie tested the water, ensuring it tasted okay.

"Take a sip," she whispered, tilting Elle's head.

"Any news?" Blue Eyes asked as he set his gun on the table.

"It's not looking good," the other man said, leaning back in his chair. "The Feds are on his tail."

"So, the idiot didn't call off his dogs. Stupid man." Blue Eyes shook his head.

Dixie swallowed the sob, smacking the back of her throat.

The other man pulled out a phone… Kent's phone.

A glimmer of hope spread like jam across Dixie's skin. She never turned off location sharing on her phone, so if Kent had found hers, he could track his and send help. Maybe they were hiding somewhere outside right now.

"We can't let the Feds nail him, especially if he still has all the product with him," the tissue man said. "Boss wants to let Danny boy think he's getting away with it right up to when he meets with whomever his buyer is, killing two birds with one stone."

"Based on Daniel's direction, I bet it's that dipshit out in Tennessee who snagged a small shipment last year," Blue Eyes said.

Tissue Man traced his thumb and forefinger across his jaw. "We need to know what the Feds are up to." He pointed to Dixie. "What do you know about all this?"

"Nothing," she croaked out.

"And your boyfriend?" Tissue Man asked.

She swallowed. Kent knew more than she did about whatever Daniel was up to, but she didn't know how much or if she should say anything. She didn't want to make matters worse. "I really don't know."

"Get him on the phone." Tissue Man chucked the phone in her direction.

"But this isn't my cell."

"Doesn't mean you can't reach him," Tissue Man said.

"What are you waiting for?" Blues Eyes picked up the gun and pointed it at her.

She fumbled with the phone, dropping it twice, trying to remember the passcode.

"9845," Elle whispered.

Sucking in a deep breath, she called her cell, praying Kent would answer.

He did on the first ring.

"Dixie? Are you okay? Is Elle okay?"

"Put it on speaker." Tissue Man pushed back his chair and stomped across the room.

"We're okay," Dixie said, setting the phone on the table. "Scared."

"Elle. Can Elle hear me?"

"Daddy!" Elle cried.

"That's enough," Tissue Man ordered. "Tell me what you know about the Feds tailing Daniel."

"I don't know anything," Kent's voice boomed from the speaker.

"We don't believe you, and unless you want to me to start cutting off fingers and toes, you better get straight with us," Blue Eyes said.

Elle whimpered, hugging Dixie in a death grip.

"Shhhhh, sweetie."

"You touch my kid, and I'll kill you," Kent said. "That's not a threat. It's a promise."

"Tell me what I want to know, and no harm will come to her," Tissue Man said with a much calmer voice.

Dixie didn't believe that statement for a second. Her stomach twisted and churned like she'd downed a jug of bad milk. She needed to find a way to get her and Elle out of this house, and soon.

"All I know was that when my contact started tailing Daniel, the FBI was already on him. That's all I know."

"All right. Your guy still nearby?" Tissue Man asked.

"He backed off, but can't be more than thirty minutes away," Kent said.

"What are you doing?" Blue Eyes said in a hushed tone.

Tissue Man waved him off.

"Put him back on. We're going to create a diversion. I'll be in touch." Tissue Man bent down and tapped the screen.

"What the fuck are you doing?" Blue Eyes furrowed his forehead.

"Making sure Daniel gets to the buyer, like our boss wants."

"Motherfucker!" Kent whipped the phone across the room, missing Arthur's head by a mere inch.

"Calm down," Arthur said with a level voice. Arthur never cracked under pressure, not even when his wife had been kidnapped and then in a car crash where Arthur had to pull her limp body from the wreckage. "Destroying her phone isn't going to help us."

Kent sucked in a breath. That phone had been their lifeline to Elle and Dixie. One good thing that came from his overprotective ways.

Arthur picked up the phone. "Still working."

Thank God.

"We're missing something," Buddy said from the kitchen table at Arthur's house near the marina and closer to where Elle and Dixie were being held. "Why would they want us to put a PI back on Daniel?"

"My guess would be they want to use our guy as a diversion. If Daniel has a buyer for the drugs, they probably want to take them both out, making a statement," Arthur said.

"Nope. That's not it." Rex walked into the kitchen carrying his laptop. "Darius got ahold of the field agent in charge of the Pepe Hernandez case, and it would appear they have an undercover agent." Rex flipped the computer screen so everyone could see. "This guy is Special Agent Simon Gant."

"That's one of the men who took Elle and Dixie." A feeling of butterflies fluttered in his stomach.

"Text just came in from your phone," Arthur said, his lips slightly smiling.

"Looks like this undercover operative just sent us their location and a time to be there. He's setting something up."

"He say anything else?" Kent asked, his pulse racing. This was all good news, but he couldn't relax until Elle and Dixie were back in his arms.

"Yeah. We're not to contact him," Arthur said.

"Well, that makes sense." Kent took the phone with a shaky hand. "Let's go."

"Dixie?" Elle's voice trembled.

"What is it, sweetie?" Dixie cupped her chin, pressing her lips against her temple.

"I have to use the bathroom."

So did Dixie, but she didn't dare ask. Blue Eyes kept pacing, constantly questioning the decisions Tissue Man made, and a few times Blue Eyes mentioned something about sending a message by chopping off a couple of fingers or toes and sending them to Kent. Tissue Man didn't like that idea, thank God, but Dixie didn't think she and Elle were going to make it out of this situation unharmed. She prayed they'd still be at least breathing.

"Um, excuse me?" she said softly.

"Shut the fuck up," Blue Eyes snapped.

Elle sniffled.

"What is it?" Tissue Man asked.

"We need to use the bathroom."

"Too bad," Blue Eyes said, laughing.

"You're an asshole, you know that?" Tissue Man waved her over. "The bathroom is over here."

"They can't go in there alone." Blue Eyes lifted the gun off the table again, waving it around. "I don't know why we don't just kill them now. We're going to anyway."

Dixie bit back a sob, but Elle couldn't keep quiet.

"Go outside to the van and get me a pack of smokes." Tissue Man pointed to the empty pack on the table. "I'll deal with the bathroom break."

"You go get them, and I'll take the girls to the bathroom. They'll have to leave the door open, and I'll have to stand over them, especially the hot mom." This time Blue Eyes waved the gun in the direction of Tissue Man.

"Boss put me in charge, so do what I say, or I'll

tell him about how you fucked up the surveillance in the first place."

Blue Eyes narrowed his eyes. "That wasn't all my fault."

Dixie helped Elle to her feet while Blue Eyes stomped out of the house.

Tissue Man looked over his shoulder several times and then raced to her side.

She pushed Elle behind her back.

"I'm not going to hurt you. We have only a few minutes. I'm an undercover federal agent, and I'm waiting to hear from my handler so that I can—"

Bang!

Elle screamed.

Tissue Man's eyes widened as he arched his back, falling to his knees.

"Knew there was something wrong with you." Blue Eyes raised the gun at Dixie.

Her body trembled as her gaze went from the man groaning on the ground and the other man inching his way forward with a sinister smile.

Think. Think.

What would Kent do? What would her father have done in a situation like this?

Kent bolted from the car the second he heard the gunshot, followed by an ear-piercing scream. His heart nearly stopped, picturing Elle lying on the ground with a bullet in her body.

Or Dixie.

Or both.

"Kent," Arthur yelled.

"Nothing you can say or do that will stop me from charging in." Kent glanced over his shoulder.

"Didn't expect you to, but I'm not letting you go alone or unarmed." Arthur's feet hit the pavement as he carried two weapons in his hand. "I'll take the front; you go around back."

"I've got the north side," Rex yelled as he ran past.

Kent did his best to push all negative thoughts from his mind. He tried to calm his pulse to something close to a normal combat situation, though he was more used to running into a burning building with a hose, not a hostile situation with a gun.

Not that he hadn't done it a time or two with the Aegis Network.

He pressed his back to the side of the house, peering into the backyard. An old door, barely hanging on the hinges, swayed, making a creaking noise. The noise would help. He peeked into the window, and his heart sank to the pit of his gut.

Elle stood behind Dixie, her face buried in her back, while Dixie stared down the wrong end of a pistol. The undercover agent was on the floor, bleeding, trying to move but couldn't. Kent couldn't tell where he'd been hit, but the look on his face, and the way his legs remained still while he withered his upper body, told Kent it wasn't good.

The man with the scar, which they now knew went by the name Dune Dog, grabbed Dixie by the neck, pressing the gun against her temple, and licked her cheek.

Kent swallowed the bile that smacked the back of his throat. If he had a clear shot, he'd take it, but it was too risky. That motherfucker was going to get hurt for doing that. Kent ducked down, inching toward the back door, trying not to make a sound, sidestepping a few twigs. He'd be able to get in undetected, but based on the angle of the kitchen, he'd be seen the second he approached the table.

There was no way either of his buddies could enter through the front door without being seen, so hopefully one of them had found access through a window somewhere.

Gently, he stepped through the door, weapon on the ready.

"You're a pretty little thing," Dune Dog said.

The way his voice cooed made Kent want to vomit.

"Nice tits too."

Kent let out a short breath through his nose. It was now or never. Inching behind the table, staying low, he made eye contact with Dixie who had turned her head, tears streaming down her cheek while that asshole had his slimy lips on her neck and his hand on her breast. Her arms were behind her, wrapped around Elle.

"Don't do this in front of her," Dixie said.

"It will be good for her to learn." Dune Dog traced the gun down the side of Dixie's face while he sniffed her hair.

Kent pointed to his gun, then at the one in Dune Dog's hand.

Dixie's eyes went wide. Hopefully, she knew what he wanted and that it would work.

"Back away from the—"

"What the fuck?" Dune Dog jerked his head around.

"Now," Kent commanded.

Dixie curled her fingers around the gun and

yanked it free from a stunned Dune Dog. She stumbled backward, shoving Elle out of the way.

"Daddy!" She raced across the room.

Dune Dog reached for Dixie.

"I wouldn't do that if I were you," Arthur said as he stepped through the front door. Rex followed, racing through the room to get to the injured man with a first aid kit. Rex was prepared for anything.

Kent set his gun on the table, holding his arms out as he pulled Elle right off the floor, squeezing her tight. His muscles ached. In a flash, he could have lost everything he loved, a feeling he hoped he'd never have to face again. "Are you hurt?"

"No," she whimpered, nuzzling her face in his neck. "I was so scared."

"I know, but Daddy's here now." Quickly, he took Elle out the back door, wanting to get her out of that house. Sirens rang out in the distance.

"Don't leave Dixie," Elle said.

"I'm not going to. Uncle Arthur is bringing her out the front door. See?"

Arthur had put Dune Dog in restraints and tied him to the railing by the front door as he helped Dixie down the front stoop.

"Your girlfriend's a feisty one," Arthur said.

"I know. I think I'll keep her." Holding his

daughter with one hand, he held out his other. "Come here."

She wiped the tears from her face and ran to him, throwing her arms around him and Elle. "Where's Nicky?" she asked, sobbing into his chest.

"He's with Tilly. When I left, he was still upset, but he promised me he'd be a big boy and hold down the fort until we got back." He kissed the top of her head. "Did that slimeball hurt you?"

She shivered. "No, but I need a long, hot shower to get the feeling of his fingers off my body."

"After we get you both checked out by a doctor."

"Elle complained of stomach pain," Dixie said.

"I'm okay," Elle whispered. "I don't need a doctor."

"Yes, you do," Dixie said with a firm tone.

Kent let out a slight laugh. "Are you being overprotective now?"

"I learned from the best." She tilted her head, staring at him with those warm, blue eyes. She glanced over her shoulder as three police cars and two ambulances pulled down the street. "I hope that man is going to be okay. He said he was a federal agent."

"He is," Arthur said as he strolled over. "Rex is tending to him now. I'm afraid it isn't looking too good. He's lost a lot of blood."

"Oh no." Elle wrapped her arms around Kent's waist.

Kent nodded toward the paramedics as they entered the house with a stretcher. A second team strolled in his direction.

"While I think Elle needs to be examined, I'm not sure another ride in an ambulance is warranted." Dixie patted his chest.

"I'll let the experts make that decision." He kissed her temple.

"I supposed that's reasonable," Dixie said.

"Oh my God." Elle rolled her eyes. "Am I going to be ganged up on by both of you now that you're an official item?"

"Consider this a nice compromise." Dixie looped her arm around Elle. "He's not making you get in the ambulance and race off to the hospital. It's better to be safe than sorry."

"I can't believe he's rubbing off on you. Next thing I know, you'll go back on your word and not take me to get a bra." Elle stomped off toward Kent's truck.

Arthur laughed. "This is my cue to go see if Rex needs anything."

Kent shifted his gaze. "You told her you'd take her shopping for bras?"

"She's getting little boobies."

"She is not." Kent stuffed his finger in his ear and wiggled. "I seriously can't believe you just said that. She's ten."

"She'll be eleven in a couple of months. Before you know it, she'll be getting her first period."

Kent reached around and covered Dixie's mouth. "I don't ever want to hear you utter those words again."

"Not saying them won't stop it from happening and you'd have to be blind not to see the way she's growing into a beautiful young woman."

Kent groaned. "I can't wait to start teaching Nicky how to pick up chicks."

Dixie laughed. "He's going to have to go to Rex or one of the other guys on how to accomplish that." She leaned into Kent's body, resting her hand on the center of his chest. "You, my friend, have no game. At all."

"Oh, I sure do. I'll show you tonight, after the kids go to bed."

"Don't go making promises you can't keep."

He heaved her to his chest, lifting her chin with his thumb and forefinger. "I'm thinking we let Nicky and Elle have a nice little sleepover. Watch a movie while you and I do some door locking." He wrinkled his forehead.

"It hurt you just to even think about letting me spend the night."

He kissed her nose. "No. Not at all. The only thing that weirded me out was how normal it felt."

11

"Let me go in first." Kent kissed his daughter's forehead.

"He's never going to change," Elle muttered.

"That's not true." Dixie took Elle by the forearm and guided her back to where Nicky sat on the floor with blocks. "Besides, he's not going in there because he's worried that man is going to hurt you or me. He's doing it because it's an honor thing."

Thank you, Kent mouthed as he turned and headed down the corridor and into Simon Grant's room. It had been three weeks since the shooting and the man was lucky to be alive. Even luckier that he would walk again.

Kent tapped his fingers against the door. "Simon? It's Kent Carter. May I come in?"

"Yes. Please. I was hoping I'd hear from you." Simon adjusted the blanket over his waist and did his best to sit up taller. "How is that precious daughter of yours? And your girlfriend and her son?"

"Everyone is doing incredibly well, considering." Kent eased into the chair by the side of the bed.

"I'm real sorry about what I had to do. I tried to find other ways to approach the situation without blowing my cover. Kidnapping your family was the last thing I wanted to do. I did my best to keep them safe, and I would have stepped in front of a bullet to save them."

"You kind of did that," Kent said with a cheeky grin. "For which I will be forever grateful."

"It's my job. It's what I signed on to do when I went undercover." Simon shrugged. "But you're no stranger to danger. Air Force. Firefighter. Aegis Network. Those are not for the faint of heart."

"No, I guess not." Kent nodded. "Listen, besides wanting to thank you personally for managing to reach me and the police and doing your best to diffuse the situation, I wanted to ask you if you would have a chat with my daughter Elle. While she's bounced back and the therapist says she's dealing with what happened incredibly well, she does occasionally have nightmares."

"I'm not surprised by the bad dreams. What happened will haunt me for as long as I live. It doesn't matter that I know I would have given up my cover if I had to in order to protect your daughter, but it doesn't change the fact there were loaded guns."

Kent took in a long breath. He wasn't over that part and it might take the rest of his life to get that image out of his head. "Oddly, that's not what she's having nightmares about."

Simon arched a brow.

"At first it was all about you dying. She'd wake up sobbing, begging me to call the hospital to check on you. Once you woke up, it became all about you slipping into a coma. For some reason, she feels responsible for what happened to you."

"That's a lot of worry for a little girl."

"Unfortunately, she gets that from her old man," Kent said. "Therapy is helping, but I thought it might do her some good to visit you. If that was okay."

"Absolutely. I'd love to visit with her. I'm sure

you don't need me to tell you what an incredible young lady you have. She was quite brave. And Dixie, she really held it together when others might have completely lost it."

"While I wished it had never happened or that I could have traded places with Dixie, I know how lucky I am that she was there and that she's in my life."

"She cared for that little girl like she was her own," Simon said.

Thick emotion gathered in Kent's throat. The bond that had developed between his daughter and Dixie was the kind of bond that couldn't—and shouldn't—be broken. He relished in watching them together as much as he enjoyed loving Nicky. It filled his heart and soul in ways he never expected. He fought the idea that bringing a woman into Elle's life would be good for them as father and child.

He'd been wrong.

But so grateful he'd waited for the right lady to stroll into his life at exactly the right time.

"Let me text Elle. She's in the waiting room with Dixie and her son down the hall."

"I'm so sorry if I scared that little boy," Simon said.

"He honestly barely remembers much. Little ones are resilient that way, but to err on the side of caution, his mother and I brought him to a pediatric psychologist who said he's adjusting to the trauma appropriately, whatever that means."

"I don't have kids, so I can't even begin to imagine what you all went through. I'm just glad it turned out the way it did."

"We're all incredibly grateful to your sacrifice and sincerely happy you're going to walk out of this hospital."

"I knew the risks when I went undercover eight months ago. It's a hard life, and I look forward to some well-deserved time off," Simon said.

"Will you go back to undercover work?"

"Probably," Simon said. "I'm not an old man and like I said, I don't have a family. It's all I know and if I can get assholes off the streets, I'm glad to do it."

Tap. Tap.

"Hi," Elle said softly as she tentatively entered the room.

Kent looped his arm around his daughter. "Simon, you remember Elle."

"I sure do." He stretched out his hand. "Thank you for the cards and flowers. They have brightened up my room and have made me feel special."

"I'm sorry that bad man shot you." Elle sat on Kent's knee—something she didn't do often anymore. "How are you feeling?"

"Pretty darn good. The doctors tell me I can go home tomorrow," Simon said.

"That's great." Elle sat up a little taller. "Do you have someone who can help take care of you?"

"I'm going to go to my sister's house to recover. Once I'm completely healed, I will take a vacation to visit my brother in Alaska. After that, it's back to work."

"I'm glad you have family to look after you." She patted the back of his hand. "But if there is anything we can do for you, I hope you'll reach out. Maybe before you leave for your trip, we can all get together. Go fishing or something."

"I'd like that." Simon nodded as the nurse came through the door.

"Come on, Elle." Kent gave her a good nudge. "We best get going. It's getting way too close to Nicky's nap time, and you know how cranky he gets when he doesn't get a good one in." He took Simon's hand in a firm shake. "Don't hesitate to call us if you need anything at all."

"And vice versa." Simon nodded.

Kent looped his arm around Elle's shoulders. "I'm so proud of you," he said once in the corridor. "You're turning into a fine young lady."

"Thanks, Daddy." She glanced up. "Does that mean I can go to the movies with Lucy and Kristen tomorrow afternoon? Without you sitting in the back of the theater?"

He laughed. "Only if I can take you girls out for pizza after."

"Don't get mad, Dad, but I'd rather Dixie take us out after. Make it a girls' thing."

Kent batted his little girl's nose. She'd forever be that in his eyes. "I suppose it won't kill me to hang out with Nicky and let you all do women stuff."

"Thanks, Daddy. I love you."

"I love you too, Buttercup."

Elle rolled her eyes.

"I'm never going to stop calling you that, but I will promise to only do it during private moments like this."

"I can live with that."

"Elle! Kent!" Nicky jumped to his feet the second they turned the corner and entered the waiting room. "Look! Look at all the blocks and what I made."

Kent leaned over. "Any idea what that is?"

"Your guess is as good as mine," Elle said.

"It's a fire station and I'm going to be a fire-fighter, just like Kent." Nicky dropped to the floor, picked up a block, and made an engine noise.

Kent tapped the center of his chest and let out a long breath. "Elle, sweetie. Would you mind playing with him for a couple of minutes? I want to talk with Dixie in the hallway for a second."

"Sure, Dad," Elle said.

In a month, his world had changed in so many ways. Sometimes, it was hard to find the right time to express his feelings, and moments passed him by.

Not today.

"Is everything okay?" Dixie asked. "Did something happen while she was visiting Simon?"

"No. That went better than I could have ever imagined. My little girl is growing up right in front of me and I get I can't stop it."

Dixie rested her hands on his shoulders and smiled. "She'll always be your little girl, even when she's married with children—"

"Let's not push it, okay?" He laughed, cupping Dixie's face. "I don't believe I've ever said this proper. Thank you for taking good care of our girl under the worst of circumstances. Knowing she was with you was the only thing that got me through that horrifying two hours." He brushed his lips over hers.

"Kent——" He pressed his finger over her lips.

"You know how much I love my baby girl. But she's not the only one I care about. Not only have I fallen head over heels for that sweet little boy of yours, but I love you. I want to watch the sunset with you in my arms and our kids by our side. I want to wake up the same way. I want to be the constant in yours and Nicky's life."

She stared at him with wide eyes. "Did you use the word *love* in reference to me?"

"I sure did."

"Wow," she whispered.

"Is that all you have to say? Are you going to leave me hanging like that with my heart in my hand?"

"Interesting place to make a major declaration. I thought something like would have been done after a nice ride into the sunset on your Harley." She smiled as bright as the burning sky scorched with dazzling oranges and reds as the sun sprinkled its rays over the earth.

He wrapped his arms around her body, heaving her against his chest. "I've wanted to say it for days, but finding the perfect moment isn't easy with two kids underfoot all the time." He arched a brow. This felt right, and I couldn't let another minute go by without saying it. So, do I get to hear the words back?"

"I don't know. I mean, I feel like I need to write a six-page document on how to date a lady properly because you suck." She palmed his cheek. "But you get an A for effort and yes, I love you right back."

"Finally," Elle said, appearing in the hallway with Nicky on her hip. "You two are painful to watch sometimes."

"No one gave you permission to come out here." Kent lifted Dixie's chin with his thumb and forefinger. "Now go back in the waiting room because your father is going to do something gross."

"Pleeeaassse," Elle said. "You think you're so good at hiding all your kissy-kissy moments from us, but you're not. We see it all the time. And for the record, it's mostly not gross. Now get it over with so we can go home." She breezed past him, stopping at the elevator and glancing over her shoulder. "And we could make this all easier if the two of you would agree to live together. Sneaking around is childish." The elevator dinged. "I'll see you downstairs in the lobby." She disappeared.

Kent dropped his forehead against Dixie's and groaned. "Did my daughter just say all that?"

"She did. Looks like someone really needs to talk with her about the birds and the bees."

"Perhaps that should come from the woman in her life." He kissed Dixie's warm lips.

"I'm happy to chat with her, but two perspectives are better than one." Dixie took his hand and tugged. "Having a dad she can talk to about anything is a gift that only you can give her and it's one she'll cherish for the rest of her life."

"I don't know what I'd do without you," he said. "It's my honor to love you."

EPILOGUE

K ent sat on the front stoop of the new home he'd bought for his family, twirling his wedding ring, staring at two envelopes next to him. Nicky, now five and about to start kindergarten, rode his big wheel around the cul-de-sac, chasing Elle. He couldn't believe she was twelve. It seemed like just yesterday he was changing her diapers, and now he was fending off boys and watching her put on a tinge of mascara.

"Hey, you," a voice sweeter than honey rang out from behind him. "You've been quiet all morning. What's going on?" Dixie sat down beside him, resting her hand on her growing belly. In just four months, they'd be adding another child to their brood. His life was almost complete.

"The paperwork came to enroll Nicky in kindergarten yesterday."

"Oh, good. I've been waiting for that." Dixie tapped his thigh. "But I know you and that's not what's on your mind. What's bugging you?"

"Nicky has been calling me *Dad* for over a year, and we've never told him otherwise."

"Elle started calling me *Mom*, and we don't correct her. We decided to be a family, and that's exactly what we are." She jerked her head. "Are you bothered by Elle calling me Mom? I know I can't take the place—"

"Sweetheart, it's not that. The first time it slipped out of Elle's mouth, it shocked me, but it warmed my heart and while I've never pressured her, I've encouraged it. She knows who gave birth to her. I'll never take that away."

"Neither will I," Dixie said. "Are you feeling differently about Nicky? I don't talk about his biological father, and I don't want to. It's a different situation," she said defensively.

"I love Nicky. He's my son in every way, which is what has me so quiet this morning." He swallowed. Hard. He knew his wife and while she might agree with what he wanted to do, she wasn't going to be happy with what he'd done. "I want Nicky to go into school with my last name. I want to officially adopt him."

Dixie gasped.

He tilted his head. Her eyes grew teary. "We'd have to contact Daniel, and I don't want to ever have that man—"

He hushed her with a quick kiss. "I beg of you not to be mad, but I had a lawyer visit him in prison, and he's agreed to give up his parental rights." He rested one of the envelopes on her lap. "He's signed all the papers. All I need is for you to agree."

"You did what? Behind my back?"

"Honey—"

"Don't honey me. You should have told me," she said with a scowl, folding her arms. "We went through so much to get Daniel out of our lives. He could have made this so difficult."

"I know." He nodded.

"And it's not something you should have gone through alone."

"I didn't want you to get your hopes up, only for Daniel to say no."

She took the envelope and opened it. "But he

didn't. He agreed." She cupped his cheek. "I should be mad, but it's the sweetest thing you've ever done for me. For our family."

"I'm glad you agree." His heart hammered in his chest. "There is one more thing."

"What's that?"

He cringed. "I talked to Elle and she agrees; you should officially adopt her too."

She made a weird screeching noise, covering her mouth.

"I know I should have had this discussion with you before I went ahead—"

She grabbed his face, planting a wet kiss on his mouth. "This is better than a stolen moment on the Harley at sunset."

"I love you," he said.

"I love you more."

"Not possible." He rubbed his hand over her swollen belly.

"We could go on like this all day."

"I have no problem with that," he said, bending over and kissing her stomach. "If I could, I'd burn how I love you into the evening sky."

Thank you for reading *Kent's Honor.* Feel free to leave an honest review!

Grab a glass of vino, kick back, relax, and let the
romance roll in…

*Sign up for my <u>Newsletter (https://dl.bookfunnel.com/
82gm8b9k4y)</u> where I often give away free books before
publication.*

*Join my private <u>Facebook group</u> (https://www.facebook.
com/groups/191706547909047/) where I post exclusive
excerpts and discuss all things murder and love!*

ABOUT THE AUTHOR

ABOUT THE AUTHOR

Jen Talty is the *USA Today* Bestselling Author of Contemporary Romance, Romantic Suspense, and Paranormal Romance. In the fall of 2020, her short story was selected and featured in a 1001 Dark Nights Anthology.

Regardless of the genre, her goal is to take you on a ride that will leave you floating under the sun with warmth in your heart. She writes stories about broken heroes and heroines who aren't necessarily looking for romance, but in the end, they find the kind of love books are written about :).

She first started writing while carting her kids to one hockey rink after the other, averaging 170 games per year between 3 kids in 2 countries and 5 states. Her first book, IN TWO WEEKS was originally published in 2007. In 2010 she helped form a publishing company (Cool Gus Publishing) with *NY*

Times Bestselling Author Bob Mayer where she ran the technical side of the business through 2016.

Jen is currently enjoying the next phase of her life…the empty nester! She and her husband reside in Jupiter, Florida.

Grab a glass of vino, kick back, relax, and let the romance roll in…

Sign up for my *Newsletter (https://dl.bookfunnel.com/ 82gm8b9k4y)* where *I* often give away free books before publication.

Join my private Facebook group (https://www.facebook. com/groups/191706547909047/) where I post exclusive excerpts and discuss all things murder and love!

Never miss a new release. Follow me on Amazon:amazon.com/author/jentalty

And on Bookbub: bookbub.com/authors/jen-talty

ALSO BY JEN TALTY

Brand new series: SAFE HARBOR!

Mine To Keep

Mine To Save

Mine To Protect

Mine to Hold

Mine to Love

Check out LOVE IN THE ADIRONDACKS!

Shattered Dreams

An Inconvenient Flame

The Wedding Driver

Clear Blue Sky

Blue Moon

Before the Storm

NY STATE TROOPER SERIES (also set in the Adirondacks!)

In Two Weeks

Dark Water

Deadly Secrets

Murder in Paradise Bay

To Protect His own

Deadly Seduction

When A Stranger Calls

His Deadly Past

The Corkscrew Killer

First Responders: A spin-off from the NY State Troopers series

Playing With Fire

Private Conversation

The Right Groom

After The Fire

Caught In The Flames

Chasing The Fire

Legacy Series

Dark Legacy

Legacy of Lies

Secret Legacy

Emerald City

Investigate Away

Sail Away

Fly Away

Flirt Away

Colorado Brotherhood Protectors

Fighting For Esme

Defending Raven

Fay's Six

Darius' Promise

Yellowstone Brotherhood Protectors

Guarding Payton

Wyatt's Mission

Corbin's Mission

Candlewood Falls

Rivers Edge

The Buried Secret

Its In His Kiss

Lips Of An Angel

Kisses Sweeter than Wine

A Little Bit Whiskey

It's all in the Whiskey

Johnnie Walker

Georgia Moon

Jack Daniels

Jim Beam

Whiskey Sour

Whiskey Cobbler

Whiskey Smash

Irish Whiskey

The Monroes

Color Me Yours

Color Me Smart

Color Me Free

Color Me Lucky

Color Me Ice

Color Me Home

Search and Rescue

Protecting Ainsley

Protecting Clover

Protecting Olympia

Protecting Freedom

Protecting Princess

Protecting Marlowe

Fallport Rescue Operations

Searching for Madison

Searching for Haven

DELTA FORCE-NEXT GENERATION

Shielding Jolene

Shielding Aalyiah

Shielding Laine

Shielding Talullah

Shielding Maribel

Shielding Daisy

The Men of Thief Lake

Rekindled

Destiny's Dream

Federal Investigators

Jane Doe's Return

The Butterfly Murders

THE AEGIS NETWORK

The Sarich Brother

The Lighthouse

Her Last Hope

The Last Flight

The Return Home

The Matriarch

Aegis Network: Jacksonville Division

A SEAL's Honor

Talon's Honor

Arthur's Honor

Rex's Honor

Kent's Honor

Aegis Network Short Stories

Max & Milian

A Christmas Miracle

Spinning Wheels

Holiday's Vacation

The Brotherhood Protectors

Out of the Wild

Rough Justice

Rough Around The Edges

Rough Ride

Rough Edge

Rough Beauty

The Brotherhood Protectors

The Saving Series

Saving Love

Saving Magnolia

Saving Leather

Hot Hunks

Cove's Blind Date Blows Up

My Everyday Hero – Ledger

Tempting Tavor

Malachi's Mystic Assignment

Needing Neor

Holiday Romances

A Christmas Getaway

Alaskan Christmas

Whispers

Christmas In The Sand

Heroes & Heroines on the Field

Taking A Risk

Tee Time

A New Dawn